Praise for Leslie Kelly

"Leslie Kelly is a rising star of romance!"
—#1 *New York Times* bestselling author
Debbie Macomber

"Kelly is a top writer,
and this is another excellent book. 4 ½ stars."
—*RT Book Reviews* on *Play with Me*

"A hip contemporary romance
packed with great one-liners! 4 ½ stars."
—*RT Book Reviews* on *Terms of Surrender*

"*One Wild Wedding Night* features sexy and
fun stories with likable characters, only to
end with a sexy story that floors me with how well
it resonates with me. Oh, this one is definitely wild,
but even better, it also aims for the heart."
—*Mrs. Giggles*

"Whoa, baby, *Overexposed* is hot stuff!
Ms. Kelly employs a great deal of heart and
humor to achieve balance with this incendiary
romance. Great characters, many of whom fans will
recognize, and a vibrant narrative kept this reader
glued to each and every word. *Overexposed* is
without a doubt one of the better Blaze books
I have read to date."
—*The Romance Reader's Connection*

D0388376

Dear Reader,

Although I've written many books for Harlequin Blaze, the ones readers most often ask me about are the Santori stories. Something about that big Italian family in Chicago just strikes a chord with people. I can't tell you how often I'm asked if I ever plan to go back and show where the family is now and how everybody is doing.

I've thought about it for a long time—these beloved characters are never far from my thoughts. How are Lottie and Simon doing? Is he still dark and haunted? What about Izzie and Nick—any chance the stripper and the bouncer ever had kids? Believe me, I'm just as curious as some of you.

So, when I started working on a sequel to *Waking Up to You,* and decided I wanted the hero to be a firefighter from Chicago, I couldn't help but think he had to be a Santori. He's not a sibling of the first six, he's a cousin. But believe me, I loved Leo Santori just as much as I did all those originals.

Fortunately, Leo has two brothers, too! And lots and lots of cousins.

I do hope you enjoy Leo and Madison's story. Thank you for your constant support.

Happy reading!

Leslie Kelly

Lying in Your Arms

—

Leslie Kelly

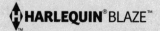

Recycling programs
for this product may
not exist in your area.

ISBN-13: 978-0-373-79771-4

LYING IN YOUR ARMS

Copyright © 2013 by Leslie A. Kelly

Printed in U.S.A.

ABOUT THE AUTHOR

Leslie Kelly has written dozens of books and novellas for Harlequin Blaze, Temptation and Harlequin HQN. Known for her sparkling dialogue, fun characters and steamy sensuality, she has been honored with numerous awards, including a National Reader's Choice Award, a Colorado Award of Excellence, a Golden Quill and a *RT Book Reviews* Career Achievement Award in Series Romance. Leslie has also been nominated four times for the highest award in romance fiction, the RWA RITA® Award.

Leslie lives in Maryland with her own romantic hero, Bruce, and their daughters. Visit her online at www.lesliekelly.com or at her blog, www.plotmonkeys.com.

Books by Leslie Kelly

HARLEQUIN BLAZE

To get the inside scoop on Harlequin Blaze and its talented writers, be sure to check out blazeauthors.com.

To my sisters, Lynn, Donna, Karen and Cheri.
You are all always in my heart.

Prologue

The Hollywood Tattler—
Shane Going NC-17?

WELL, LADIES, GET *ready to indulge in a sexy lovefest with superhot movie star Tommy Shane. Word is circulating that Shane's fiancée, screenwriter Madison Reid, is on the verge of selling her naughtily-ever-after screenplay and her hubby-to-be is going to star in it!*

Shane, who regularly lands on everyone's sexiest men alive lists, has played action heroes, romantic leads and innocent soldiers. But my sources tell me this next role—as a mysterious, dangerous man who lures an innocent young woman into his dark sexual fantasies—will be the edgiest, hottest performance of his career.

As if women all over the world didn't already have enough to fantasize about when it came to this golden-haired Adonis.

Soon, fantasizing will be all other women can do. Because we're also hearing rumors that Tommy and his fiancée have finally started making wedding plans for next year. Although Shane and Reid—his childhood sweetheart—live in a swanky beachside house in Laguna, they're heading to the other coast for the nuptial celebration. They will reportedly be having a small, private ceremony with their families in Florida, where they grew up as next-door neighbors.

Can you imagine Thomas Superstud Shane being the boy next door? Be still my heart.

We don't know a whole lot about the beautiful Miss Reid. But we suspect millions of women around the world would give anything and everything to be in her shoes. Or at least in her bed. I mean, who doesn't want to know just how much of her sultry screenplay is based on her real-life adventures with Tommy!

Congratulations and good luck you gorgeous lovebirds. I'll be watching the mail for my invitation.

1

"WAIT, ARE YOU SAYING you *want* me to break up with you?"

Not sure she'd correctly heard the drop-dead gorgeous man sitting across from her, Madison waited for a response from Tommy Shane. Aka her fiancé, aka the handsomest man alive, aka Superstud, aka Academy Award nominee.

Aka the man who wanted *her* to dump *him* right after they'd intentionally leaked details about their hush-hush wedding.

Aka…WTF?

"Yeah, Mad. I do."

She didn't get angry, the way most fiancées probably would. She wasn't the typical fiancée and theirs wasn't a typical relationship. Not by a long shot. If they knew the truth, most people would say she and Tommy put the "dys" in dysfunctional.

So, no, she wasn't angry. She was just confused, not sure what was going on. "You're the one who wanted this engagement."

"I know."

"You're the one who leaked the wedding date to the press."

"I know that, too."

"You're the one who played up the childhood-sweethearts-going-home-to-Florida-to-get-married angle."

"Yes."

"You convinced me to leave New York and move out here."

He shook his head. "But you're glad about that, aren't you? Look how well you're doing. Any day now, you're going to get a call that one of the big studios is going to produce your screenplay."

She wished she could be as sure. Madison had confidence in the story she'd crafted and pitched to the studios, with Tommy's help. But that didn't make it a done deal, even with his name attached to it as the star. Although, that sure didn't hurt.

She hadn't written it with him in mind. She'd seen her possibly murderous hero being someone much more dark and twisted. But he'd read the script, loved it and asked for the role. Who was she to turn down Hollywood's number one box office draw?

"This isn't simply cold feet, is it?" she asked, glancing down at the feet in question. "Make that cold ginormous feet."

"They're warm and toasty," he said with a flirtatious grin that would melt the underwear off any woman. Well, any woman who didn't know him well. "And you know what they say, big feet…"

"Big, fat ego," she said with a definite eye roll. Tommy Shane had long ago lost the ability to flirt his way around her common sense. She liked him—loved him, in fact—but she was wise to his antics and not susceptible to his looks or his charm.

"So, what do you say? Will you dump me, ASAP, preferably in as public a manner as possible?"

"Dude, seriously? I'd be happy to dump you on your ass so hard your butt cheeks will look like pancakes," she said, feeling far more relieved than a supposedly blushing bride should. "But I have two questions. First, will anybody buy it?"

"Huh?"

"I mean, why would any woman ever break up with you?"

"Well, I'm gay."

There was that.

Tommy's legion of worldwide fans wouldn't believe it, but his sexuality hadn't been a secret to her, not for a long time. He might play the part of sex symbol to every woman on the planet, but in his private life, Tommy Shane was strictly attracted to men—lately one particular man—and was very happy about it.

"Yeah, but nobody knows about that. Wasn't your in-the-closet-ness the reason we got engaged in the first place?"

"Of course."

"And haven't we been playing lovebirds to the press to cement your cover story so you can keep those sexy-leading-man roles coming your way?"

He smirked. "Well, it wasn't for your smoking-hot bod."

Chuckling, she placed a hand against her smoking-hot hip, knowing she held as much sex appeal for him as a beach ball. The one time she'd tried to kiss him romantically—when they were in middle school—she'd known they lacked any chemistry. It hadn't taken her long to figure out why. Hell, she should have figured it out in elementary school when the two of them would always fight over who got to be Buttercup when they played Powerpuff Girls.

Although the story they'd fed to the press had been fairy-tale nonsense, there had been some truth in it. They had known each other from childhood. She, Tommy and her twin sister Candace—who'd always played Bubbles to their Buttercup during *The Power-puff Girls* days—had been inseparable growing up. He'd climbed into their window for secret sleepovers, had spent long summer days with them at the beach. He had taught Candace how to dance, and Madison how to give a blow job…using a banana, of course. He'd always loved to perform, but had also been strong—he even punched a guy once who'd groped Madison at a concert. Heck, he'd been the one who'd bought a pregnancy test kit for her when she'd had a late-period scare in high school. He'd even offered to marry her if the stick turned blue!

He was a wonderful, loyal, devoted friend. Which was why she had stepped in and agreed to get engaged to him in his time of need…after her sister, who was *supposed* to be the false fiancée, had gone and fallen in love with her dream man.

No, the engagement wasn't supposed to culminate in a real marriage, but their planned breakup was a long way off. They'd scheduled everything, figuring in shooting schedules and premieres, knowing how long they needed to keep up the pretense. They'd discussed how to pull off a gradual, *friendly* breakup once both of them were in good enough career positions to come out of it unscathed. And now he wanted to ditch all that in favor of an impromptu dumping, before they'd even had a chance to stage a public disagreement?

"Nobody'll buy it. You're the biggest fish in the ocean. What woman in her right mind would let you slip off her hook?"

"They'll believe it once the world knows what a cheating mackerel I am," he said with a simple shrug.

She gaped. "Tell me you're joking. You did not cheat!"

She didn't add *on me*. How could he cheat on her when they weren't involved? Even if the big rock on her finger said otherwise.

But there was someone else he could have cheated on, which would break Madison's heart. Tommy's new guy was wonderful.

"You didn't betray Simon, did you?"

"No, of course not," he insisted, looking horrified.

That made her feel a little better. Tommy wasn't the most reliable sort when it came to his romantic life. If he was stupid enough to screw up this new relationship, she'd personally whack him upside the head with his own SAG Award.

"So you two are still okay?"

"Fine." Tommy smiled wistfully. "He's great, isn't he?"

"More than great." Simon, a neurosurgeon, made her friend happier than she'd seen him in years. "So who'd you cheat on?"

"You."

"You're saying you have another best-friend-turned-fake-fiancée…besides Candace? I mean, I've always forgiven you for cheating on me with my sister, even when we were in third grade and you always picked her first for kick ball."

"Not Candace," he said. "I meant, you tell the world I cheated on you. Since I'm turning over an open-and-honest leaf, you don't even have to say it was with a woman. That'll just be what people will think. Who wouldn't dump me for cheating?"

Huh. He had a point. Technically, that was true.

"People will buy it. We'll be all Rob-and-Kristen-like."

She caught the reference. Madison wasn't a Hollywood insider, despite her engagement to a crown prince of Tinseltown, but who hadn't heard of the scandal surrounding one of Hollywood's "It" couples during the whole *Twilight* craze?

"Okay, so they probably would believe that. People have been wondering how on earth I caught you in the first place."

"Don't sell yourself short, gorgeous."

She shrugged. Attractive? Yeah, she'd cop to that. But gorgeous? No way. She had never felt more inept and lacking as a woman than when she'd attended some of these L.A. parties packed wall-to-wall with women who were pretzel-stick thin, cover-girl perfect and runway model clothed. Oh, and saber-toothed-tiger clawed. Sheesh, the competition out here was insane.

"But even if it works, *why* should we do it now rather than sticking to our long engagement, slow-breakup plan?"

He thrust a hand through his thick, sun-streaked hair, looking boyishly adorable. If there'd been an audience, all the women would just have sighed, every one of them dying to smooth that soft hair back into place. Madison just grunted.

Melodrama over, he said, "It's because of Simon."

"He asked you to do this?"

"No. We've been talking about how important it is to be honest. Me living a lie with you—no matter how good the reason or the fact that you're fine with it— won't convince him I'm growing and becoming true to myself."

"Simon would never want you to sabotage your career."

"I know. But this is a step toward the kind of life I want, and the kind of man I want to be. One who isn't afraid, who doesn't go to crazy lengths to hide who he is."

She rarely heard Tommy talk this way. His blue eyes didn't sparkle with mischief. He didn't appear to be acting. He was just being the sweet boy next door she'd always known, telling her what he really wanted, all the pretense stripped away, all the trappings of his life-style shoved into the background. Just Tommy. Just her friend. Her friend who needed her.

She'd always been there when he needed her, and vice versa.

"Besides, you're not being true to yourself, either," he added. "You aren't like Candace. I knew it wouldn't be a hardship for her to go without sex for a while. You, though… I know you're horny enough to climb out of your own skin."

She couldn't deny that; Tommy knew her well. She'd been the first one of the three of them to lose her virginity—at sixteen—and had probably had more lovers than the other two combined. The six months of their engagement had been the longest she'd gone without sex in *years,* and her biggest, naughtiest toys just weren't filling the gap anymore. So to speak.

"You've been a great fiancée. Now you can be off the hook and go out there and *get* some."

"Sure, I'll just find a hot guy and say, 'Do me, baby.'"

"Yep."

"Not so easy."

"Not so hard, either. So, will you dump me? Free us both?"

Hell, she'd gotten engaged to him out of love, hadn't she? Of course she could dump the man for the same reason.

But, she suddenly realized, dumping him might not be in his best interest. Because here was the thing about movie star breakup scandals. It was always the cheater who got slammed, not the cheatee. Frankly, Madison didn't need public approval. They wouldn't pay one moment's attention to a wannabe screenwriter who'd had a fling.

But Tommy Shane? Every woman's fantasy man, every kid's comic book hero, every man's wanna-be-him guy? Well, hell. Tommy Shane couldn't be a cheater. It would be like…like John Wayne turning out to be a secret communist or something.

"We can do this," she told him, slowly thinking it out. "But I have a condition of my own."

"I'll still pay you half of everything I made this year."

"Forget the money." She'd never take another dime from him. Tommy had supported her while she'd finished her screenplay. He'd helped her pay her student loans. And she'd let him, figuring if she was going to give up her life, her job, her home and any other man for the duration of their engagement, she would earn it. She was not coming out of this relationship grasping the short end of the stick.

But she was almost free now. That was worth more than money. She'd gone into this with her eyes open, and didn't regret it, but she couldn't deny a big part of her was ready to be just Madison Reid, writer, not Tommy Shane's fiancée.

And, though she wouldn't admit it, getting to have sex again was a pretty darned big perk, too.

"So what's your condition?" he asked.

"The condition is…I take the heat."

"Huh?"

"I'm the cheater. I'm the bitch. And you break up with me."

He sputtered. "No, you can't do that."

She put a hand up, cutting off his arguments. "Tommy Shane can't be a cheating dog. I can. Nobody'll give a damn."

"You don't know that," he said. "The press can be nasty."

"Why would they? They'll say I'm an idiot for letting you get away and that'll be the end of it."

"What if it's not?"

"Well, then, I'll…take a vacation. You send me somewhere tropical and I'll hide out until they forget all about me."

"You should do that anyway. Find a nice, hunky beach bum to shack up with for a little while," he said with an eyebrow wag.

"I'll think about it. So we're agreed?"

He frowned, clearly not liking the idea, but she wasn't going to change her mind. Tommy would never get through a scandal unscathed, but she would. Who cared about Madison Reid? She could take whatever heat anybody wanted to dish out because it wouldn't last for long.

And if it did? Well…there was always the somewhere-tropical-with-a-hunky-beach-bum idea.

2

"It's going to be one hell of a honeymoon."

Although the driver of the cab looked confused, considering Leo Santori was sitting alone in the backseat, he didn't reply. And it wasn't just because this was Costa Rica and Leo didn't speak Spanish. The driver spoke English, or something very much like it. No, he just seemed to be abiding by the code that said Americans on vacation in tropical paradises could be as strange as they wanted to be. It was all good. No problem.

"All good. No problem," Leo muttered.

All good that he was honeymooning alone.

No problem that he'd been betrayed.

It's really all good that my fiancée cheated on me six months ago so we canceled the wedding, which was supposed to have taken place yesterday. No problem that she kept the ring, the apartment, her yappy bichon frise—which really was *no problem—and the new KitchenAid mixer, and I kept the nonrefundable honeymoon.*

She'd also kept the best man. The one she'd cheated with.

No problem.

Still, it certainly was not a conversation he wanted to have with anyone. Especially not now that he was here in Central America, ready to embark on some to-hell-with-it adventures. Those would definitely include surfing and zip lining. Good drinks, beautiful beaches, exotic foods.

They also might include getting laid. *If* he happened to meet a woman who was interested in a rebound-sex-fest with a Chicago firefighter who had a slight chip on his shoulder and a honeymoon package created for two but starring only one.

"Here we are, *señor,*" said the driver.

The ride from the international airport in Liberia to this west coast paradise had been comfortable. The driver had pointed out various sights that Leo felt sure he'd explore over the next several days. No doubt about it, Costa Rica was every bit as beautiful—sunny, robin's-egg-blue skies, vivid hills and jungles, perfect eighty-degree climate—as the brochures had said. An outstanding choice for a honeymoon. Even a solo one.

"Thanks, man," he said.

The driver pulled out his suitcase and handed it off to a broadly smiling doorman who quickly swept it through the entrance of the hotel, which, as advertised, looked small, tasteful and upscale. Inside, Leo glanced around, noting that every wall seemed open to the out-doors. But it was still comfortable, a soft tropical breeze blowing through, whispering along the cool tile floors and setting the potted palms in gentle motion.

A bellhop engaged him in conversation in heavily

accented English as they walked to the check-in desk. Leo only understood half of what he said, responding with smiles and nods.

The woman at the desk greeted him. "Welcome, Mr. Santori, we're so very glad to have you with us."

She smiled, obviously noting his surprise at being called by name. Then he thought about it and realized he might very well be the only person checking in today. He remembered from the research he'd done on this place that there were only twenty-four rooms on the whole property. Twenty-four bungalows each with a small, private pool and walled garden, just the thing for a romantic interlude between a new bride and groom.

Christ, what was he doing here?

The middle-aged woman, whose English was only slightly tinged with an accent, glanced past him and looked around the open lobby. "And where is Mrs. Santori?"

He grimaced. Obviously, despite his calls and his emails, word had not filtered down to the front desk that he would be traveling alone.

"Uh…"

"Oh, dear," the woman said, reading something on the screen and biting her lip in consternation. She swallowed, visibly embarrassed. "I'm so sorry, Mr. Santori, I didn't see the notation on your reservation."

Okay, so *somebody* had paid attention when he'd changed the reservation to make it clear he was no longer traveling with a companion. It had just taken her a moment to see the note. He wondered what it said.

Maybe: *attention—pathetic sap was cheated on and didn't get married.*

He doubted it happened often, but he couldn't be the first single-on-a-honeymoon vacationer they'd ever seen.

He didn't ask her to turn the screen so he could read it. His imagination was good enough. "No problem."

She smiled her appreciation. "How was your trip from the airport, sir?"

"Fine, thanks."

"Wonderful." Her fingers continued to click on her keyboard as she finished working on his check-in. "We have you in our Emerald Bungalow. It's one of our nicest on the west side of the property. Sunsets over the Pacific will make you gasp."

Yeah. He was sure he'd be doing a lot of gasping during this trip, just not for the reasons he'd expected. It sure wouldn't be out of breathlessness from the ninety-seven ways he and Ashley would have been having sex.

He pushed her name out of his head. He'd done a great job of that for the past six months, since the day he'd mistaken her phone for his and discovered the kinds of intimate sexting pictures he'd *never* want to see from a guy. Definitely not from Tim, his own old friend…and best man. Especially not when those messages were written to—and welcomed by—Leo's fiancée.

Six months had been enough to calm the anger, soften the insult, heal the heart. For the most part. It maybe hadn't been enough to kill the embarrassment, which was what he most felt these days when he thought about it. Which wasn't often.

It was only because he'd come here, to take advantage of the nonrefundable vacation he'd paid for months before the scheduled wedding date, that he was thinking of his ex. Back home in Chicago, around his big extended family, or the guys at the station or the women wanting to help him jump back into the dating game, he was able to forget there'd ever been an Ashley. Or that he'd ever been stupid enough to think he'd *really* been in love with her. If he'd *really* been in love with her, Tim wouldn't have ended up with a broken nose—he'd have ended up in traction. Or, if his great uncle Marco—supposedly mob connected—had had his way, with a pair of cement shoes.

But no. That wasn't Leo's way. No broken legs or kneecaps, definitely nothing even worse. Ashley just hadn't been worth it. When it came right down to it, he'd known his pride had been a whole lot more bruised than his heart. So he'd walked out on her without a big scene, not moved by her crocodile tears. And he'd let Tim off with a punch in the face…and a warning to watch his wallet since Ashley was a bit of a spender.

Frankly, that was why he figured she'd gone for the guy to begin with. The one place Tim had ever outdone Leo in *anything* was the wallet. Hopefully the lawyer would continue raking in the bucks to keep Ash supplied in the stupid snowmen figurines to which she was addicted. Actually, screw it. He didn't care if she never got another one, or if the freaky-faced little monsters melted. At least he didn't have to look at them anymore.

"Sir?" the desk clerk prompted.

Realizing he'd let his mind drift, he shoved away thoughts of Ashley. He was in paradise and had no room in his head for anything dark. "Sounds great, thanks."

"Here you go," she said, handing him a plastic key-card. She also gave him a map of the property. "I hope you have a wonderful time. There are so many things to do, so many people to meet."

He needed to get away from her slightly pitying expression before she mentioned that she had a single niece or something.

The bellhop approached with his suitcase and led him out of the lobby onto a path that wound through the lush grounds. He pointed out a few conveniences including, Leo thought, directions to the pool area and the beach. Or maybe he'd been pointing out a bird or an outhouse, frankly, Leo had no idea.

Finally, they came to a stop in front of a thatch-roofed cottage. "You," the man said with a big smile.

Nodding, Leo slid his key into the reader. The light didn't turn green, and he didn't hear a click as the lock disengaged.

"Is no good?" the belhop asked.

"Doesn't appear to be."

The worker took the key card, tried himself, several times. It didn't work for him, either.

"Forget it. I'll have them reprogram it," Leo said, not happy about having to trudge back to the lobby. Right now, he just wanted to strip out of his clothes and take a cool shower.

"Here," the bellhop said, pulling out his own master keycard. That would save him the lobby trip for a while, anyway.

Following the man inside, Leo glanced around the room. It was large, airy, bright and immaculate. The vaulted ceiling was lined in pale wooden planks and two fans spun lazily overhead. Sandstone tile floors, peach walls, vibrant paintings of island life…just as advertised. A small café table designed for cozy, intimate breakfasts stood in one corner near a love seat. And the enormous king-size bed looked big enough for four honeymooners. He hid a sigh and shifted his gaze.

The bellhop lifted the suitcase onto the dresser, then headed over to unlock the patio door. He pulled it open and a warm, salt-and-flower-tinged breeze wafted in, bathing Leo's skin. He wouldn't need any AC; the ocean breezes were amazing.

"Pool, is very private," the man said.

"I can see that." Naked midnight swims had sounded appealing when they'd chosen this place. "Thank you," he said, pulling some cash out of his pocket and handing it over.

The man smiled and departed. Alone, Leo walked to the sliding door, glancing outside at the small pool, which was surrounded on all sides by a tall hedge covered with bright pink flowers. The owners had really meant it when they'd promised privacy for the pool. The resort boasted a large one, with a swim-up bar and lounge chairs, but right now, wanting that coolness on every inch of his skin, he figured this smaller one would do the trick. Midnight naked swims? Hell…

with that hedge and the stone wall behind it, daytime ones would be fine, too.

Smiling, he checked out the rest of the suite, pausing in the bathroom to strip out of his clothes and grab a towel, which he slung over one shoulder. He returned to the patio door, put one hand on the jamb and another on the slider and stood naked in the opening, letting that breeze bathe his body in coolness.

Heaven.

He was just about to step outside and let the warm late-day sun soak into his skin when he heard something very out of place. A voice. A woman's voice. Coming from right behind him...inside his room.

"Oh. My. God!"

Shocked, he swung around, instinctively yanking the towel off his shoulder and letting it dangle down the middle of his body. To cover the bits that were dangling.

A woman stood in his room, staring at him, wide-eyed and openmouthed. They stared at each other, silent, surprised, and Leo immediately noticed several things about her.

She was young—his age, maybe. Definitely not thirty.

She was uncomfortable, tired, or not feeling well. Her blouse clung to her curvy body, as if it was damp with sweat. Dark smudges cupped her red-rimmed eyes, and she'd already kicked off her shoes, which rested on the floor right by the door, as if her first desire was to get barefoot, pronto.

Oh. And she was hot. Jesus, was she ever.

Gorgeous, in fact, with honey-brown hair that fell in a long, wavy curtain over her shoulders. Although reddened, her big green eyes were sparkling, jewel-toned, heavily lashed, with gently swooping brows above. Her face was perfect—high cheekbones, pretty chin, lush mouth. That body... Well, he suddenly blessed perspiration because the way that silky blouse clung to the full curves of her breasts was enough to make his heart skip every other beat. And the tight skirt that hugged curvaceous hips and several inches of long, slim thigh—leaving the rest of her legs bare for admiring—was making it skip every one in between.

She was also something else, he suddenly realized. Shocked. Stunned. Maybe a little afraid.

"Hi," he said with a small smile. He remained where he was, not wanting to startle her.

"I... You... You're naked!"

"I am, yes."

Her green eyes moved as she shifted her attention over his body, from bare shoulders, down his chest, then toward the white towel that he clutched in his fist right at his belly. She continued staring, scraping her attention over him like a barber used a blade—close, oh so damned close, and so very edgy.

Something like comprehension washed over her face and her tensed, bunched shoulders relaxed a little bit. "Did Tommy send you?" she whispered.

"Huh?"

"Of course it was Tommy. Or Candace? But, wait, this isn't... I'm not... Look, I don't need you."

"Don't need me for what?" *To do your taxes? Cut your hair? Carry your suitcase?*

Put out your fire?

Oh, he suspected he could do that last one, and it wasn't just because of his job.

"To have sex with me. I don't need to get laid this badly."

His jaw fell open. *"What?"*

She licked her lips. "I mean, you're very attractive and all." Her gaze dropped again, and he noticed the redness in her cheeks, and the audible breaths she drew across those lush lips. "Still, I just don't do that. I couldn't."

He had no idea what she was babbling about. But he was starting to get an idea. The gentlemanly part of him wanted to tell her right away that she was in the wrong room. The *male* part demanded he wait and see what on earth this beauty would say next.

"You couldn't do what?" he asked, letting the towel drop a little bit. Oh, it still covered what he needed to cover, but he wasn't gripping it the way a spinster virgin would grip her petticoats. And when she licked her lips, eyeing the thin trail of hair that disappeared beneath the terry fabric, he couldn't resist letting it slip a little bit more.

He was no flasher. But damn, the woman made it interesting to be ogled.

Her eyes almost popped out of her head. "I couldn't, you know, uh, hire you."

He didn't ask what for. It sure wasn't to trim her hedges. At least, not any green ones. He'd begun to suspect she'd taken him for an escort…or even a gigolo. Why on earth this beautiful woman would need either one, he couldn't say. But he was having fun trying to figure it out.

"I'm not desperate. I would never, uh, have sex with a, uh, professional." Her voice falling into a mumble, she added, "Not even one with the finest male ass I have ever seen in my entire life."

Leo was torn between indignation, laughter and lust. Right now, judging by how he felt about the way her assessing eyes belied every word she said about not wanting him, lust was winning the battle.

"You wouldn't, huh?" He stepped closer, moving easily, slowly, almost gliding.

She did the same, edging closer, her bare feet sliding smoothly over the tile floor. "No. Never."

They met near the end of the bed, both stopping when they got within a couple of feet of each other. She licked her lips, shrugged her shoulders, and said, "So, thanks for the effort, it was a, um, nice surprise. But I think you should go."

"You'd like that, would you?"

Her eyes said *no*. Her lips forced out the word, "Yes."

"I can't do that," he said, his voice low, thick.

He edged closer, unable to resist lifting a hand to brush a long, drooping curl back from her face, tucking it behind her ear. She hissed a little, tilting her head, as if to curve her cheek into his palm.

"Why not?" she whispered.

His tone equally as intimate, he replied, "Because you're in my room."

She froze, eyed him, then quickly looked around. Her gaze landed on his suitcase. She turned to peer into the bathroom, obviously seeing the clothes he'd let fall to the floor. Then back at him. "Your…"

"My room," he said, a slow smile pulling his lips up.

"You mean, you're a… You're not a…"

"Right. I'm a. And I'm not a."

She groaned softly, her green eyes growing bright with moisture. Those shoulders slumped again in pure, visible weariness and her mouth twisted. She didn't look so much embarrassed as purely humiliated. Dejected.

"I'm so sorry," she muttered.

She backed up a step, obviously not realizing how close she was to the bed. Her hip banged into the wooden footboard, and she winced, jerking away and suddenly losing her balance. She tumbled to her side, toward the hard tiled floor.

Leo didn't stop to think. He lunged, diving to catch her as she fell, letting out an oomph as she landed in his arms. Her tall, slender body was pressed against his, fitting perfectly, her head tucked under his chin, her slim waist wrapped in one arm, her shoulders in the other. She didn't immediately squirm away. Instead, she stared up at him, her eyes round, her mouth rounder.

Their stares locked and he found himself trying to identify just what shade of green those beautiful eyes were. Emerald? Jade? Jungle? Something like all of the above, plus they had a tiny ring of gold near the pupil, looking like a starburst.

She said nothing, just stared at his face. The moment stretched between them, long, heavy and strange. It was as if they were communicating on a deep, elemental level, no words being necessary, saying everything two people who'd just met would usually say. Like they wanted to get the preliminaries out of the way. For what, he didn't yet know.

"Thank you," she said, breathing the words across those lush lips.

If this were a movie, his next step would be to kiss her.

If it were a steamy one, the kiss would lead to so much more. He could suddenly see himself touching her, stroking the tip of his finger down the slick column of her throat, into the V of her blouse. Flicking it open, button after button, and pulling the fabric away from her heated skin.

In a moment as long as a single heartbeat, his mind had filled in all the blanks, seeing what it would be like to touch her, make love to her, without ever even learning her name. As if she were a present who'd landed in his arms just because he deserved her.

His body reacted—how could it not react?—but the position wasn't awkward enough to make it incredibly obvious to her. But maybe she was aware, anyway. A pink flush had risen up her face and her lips had fallen apart so she could draw deep, shaky breaths. He could see the frantic racing of her pulse in her throat, and her body trembled.

Yeah. She knew. And judging by the warm, musky scent of woman that began to fill his every inhalation, he wasn't the only one affected by the shocking encounter.

There's one problem. This isn't a movie.

Right. This was real life, she was a stranger and he,

as far as he knew, was a nice guy. The woman was obviously confused, light-headed enough to fall when she moved too quickly. And she didn't look like the type to have anonymous sex with someone she'd known for five minutes.

Time to end this, he knew. Time to put her on her feet, push her out the door and hope he ran into her again this week when she was steady, healthy and fully in control of her thoughts.

God, did he hope he'd been good enough in his life to be rewarded like that.

"This is a little awkward," she finally whispered, as if realizing the cloud of lust had begun to lift from his brain and reality was returning.

"Easy for you to say. At least you have some clothes on."

A tiny gasp escaped her lips. Reflexively, she cast a quick glance down at the floor. He followed the glance, seeing the same pile of white fabric she was seeing.

His towel. He'd dropped it when he'd lunged to catch her.

Yeah. He was naked. Completely naked, aroused at the feel of hot, musky, soft woman in his arms.

A woman who looked on the verge of...

"Son of a bitch," he mumbled.

Because she was no longer on the verge of anything. The beautiful stranger had fainted.

3

MADISON HAD BEEN HAVING the strangest dream. As she slowly woke up, feeling coolness on her face, she realized she must have drifted off on the plane. The cool air had to be coming from the vent over her seat.

She shifted, but didn't open her eyes right away, liking the dream a little too much. In it, she'd already arrived at her destination—a tropical resort where she intended to hide out for a week. She'd entered her room, exhausted, sweaty, miserable and nauseous from the long cab ride—necessitated by her landing at the wrong Costa Rican airport. Just another example of how quickly she'd had to get out of the U.S., how desperate she'd been to get away.

Things hadn't gotten much better on her arrival. The doorman had been arguing with a deliveryman, the guy at the check-in desk barely spoke English and kept suggesting she wait for a woman who was apparently on break. She'd lost patience, demanding her key and dragged her own suitcase through the thickly vegetative grounds.

Arriving in her room, wanting nothing but a cold shower and bed, she'd entered, kicked off her shoes, and had been stunned to behold a naked Adonis standing with his back toward her.

That was how she knew she'd been dreaming. Men that gorgeous, that utterly perfect, didn't exist outside of dreams and fantasies. Even Tommy, admittedly one of the handsomest men alive, wasn't built like *that*.

The man's hair had been dark, almost black, short, thick and wavy. And his bare body had been a thing of art. Broad shoulders had flexed as he'd leaned in the doorway, as if wanting to soak up the outdoors. His strong back was delineated with muscle that rippled with his every movement. Smooth skin encased a slim waist and hips, and he had an unbelievably perfect butt and long, powerful legs.

He'd turned around to reveal a strong, handsome face, masculine and unforgettable. Broad of brow, with deep-set, heavily-lashed brown eyes, slashing cheekbones, jutting chin with a tiny cleft, and a sexy, half smiling mouth.

Unfortunately, her dream state hadn't left him completely uncovered in the front. Her brain had inserted a coy white towel. She wanted to dive back into the dream to see it drop. Oh, she hoped she didn't have to open her eyes before that towel dropped.

But, wait…it *had* dropped. Hadn't it? For some reason, she remembered it on the floor. But she couldn't remember if he'd let it fall as he took her into his arms to passionately kiss her or what. Stupid dream really needed to come back and fill in all the blanks. Or at least most of them. The most interesting ones. She wasn't going to let herself wake up until it did, not even if they landed and started deboarding the plane.

"Open your eyes."

She growled in her throat.

"Come on, open up. You're okay."

That voice was seriously messing with her good dream vibes. But it was, she had to concede, a nice voice. Deep, sexy, masculine. Was it a flight attendant, rousing her for landing? Or was she still dreaming about Mr. Tall, Dark and Built?

"Come on, sweetheart." Coolness brushed her temples, soft, featherlight, then her mouth. "Take a sip."

Moisture kissed her lips. Was her dream guy giving her champagne? She swallowed.

Water. Not champagne.

And that moisture on her temples was sliding down into her hairline.

And...and...this wasn't a dream.

Her eyes flew open.

Definitely not a dream.

"You," she breathed.

It had really happened. She'd arrived at the hotel, walked into her room, seen a gorgeous stranger, and, what? Fallen and hit her head or something? What other reason would there be for her to be...where was she?

It took only a second for her to gather her wits. Holy shit, she was lying flat on her back in a bed. And this handsome, bare-chested stranger was sitting right beside her, tenderly pressing a damp facecloth to her forehead, eyeing her with visible concern.

"You're okay. Take deep breaths. Drink a little more."

She obediently sipped from the water bottle he placed against her lips, trying to kick her brain back into operation.

"What happened?"

"You fainted."

"I never faint." Girlie-girls fainted, and Madison was not a girlie-girl. She'd never been the type who'd wilt like a flower, especially not in front of some man.

Some man who'd apparently picked her up, put her on the bed and taken care of her.

"There's a first time for everything."

She frowned, still having a hard time believing it.

"Why would I faint?"

"When was the last time you ate?"

"I can't remember."

"Well, that could have something to do with it."

Yes, it could.

"You don't look like you've slept much lately, either."

She couldn't remember the last time she'd had a full, uninterrupted night's sleep. "I slept on the plane. Or… maybe that was a dream of a dream. Hell, I don't know."

"You looked pretty uncomfortable when you arrived. Sick maybe."

Sick? Maybe sick at heart. Heaven knew she had reason, considering what her life had been like in recent weeks.

"Do you think you're going to be okay? Should I have the hotel call an ambulance?"

"Good heavens, no!" That was all she needed. More attention. So much for slinking unnoticed into another country and hiding from the world for a while. "I just… I was really carsick. I guess I flew into the wrong airport and it took hours to get here, with no air-conditioning and tons of twisty roads." Ugh, when she thought about all those ups, downs and hairpin turns, she felt her stomach roll over.

"You need to eat something."

It rolled again. But she knew he was right. Something light would probably be good.

She scrunched her brow, trying to recall the last time she'd sat down for a meal, and honestly couldn't remember. Crackers on the plane probably didn't count, though she'd give her right arm for some right now, if only to settle her churning stomach. Whether it was still churning from the drive here or from the fact that this gorgeous stranger was sitting close beside her on a bed, she had no idea.

"Why don't I order something from room service?"

"You don't have to do that."

"You know what they say, save someone's life and they become your responsibility."

She rolled her eyes. "Saved my life, huh?"

He smiled and a tiny dimple appeared in one cheek, taking that dish of handsome and adding a big heaping helping of freaking adorable on top.

"If I hadn't caught you, you would have cracked your head open. That tile's pretty hard."

She suddenly thought about everything that had happened before she'd tripped. The awkward conversation when she'd rejected his *services*. Services he hadn't even been offering.

The way they'd drawn closer together, even while she'd been saying no, as if some unseen magnetic pull between their bodies was working them into close proximity.

Tripping over her own stupid feet. Falling. Him catching her.

The towel on the floor.

Gasping a little, she immediately looked down, not sure whether to sigh in relief or cry in disappointment that he wasn't naked. At some point, he'd grabbed a pair of jeans and yanked them on. They weren't even buttoned, as if he'd been in too much of a hurry to do more than zip. Maybe because he'd been busy lifting her onto the bed, fetching a cold cloth and water to revive her?

She swallowed hard, her mouth dry despite the water she'd been sipping. Because she had a mad impulse to grab the tab of that zipper and pull it down a little more, to see if he'd taken the time to put on anything else before the jeans. She suspected not.

"Well, you definitely seem to be feeling better."

That deep, husky voice suddenly sounded more amused than solicitous. Madison realized what she'd done—jerking her attention off his face and ogling him like a stripper at ladies night—and gulped. She took a deep breath, then worked up the courage to look up. It was a slow lift of the eyes. She just couldn't resist focusing on his body, so close, so big and warm and spicy smelling. She had to note the flat stomach rippled with muscle, the broad chest, wiry hair encircling his flat nipples. Those powerful shoulders, corded and thick, and on up the throat to the strong, lightly grizzled jaw.

And the face. Oh, lord, that face.

That smiling face.

"You done?"

She took a deep, even breath.

"I'm a little confused," she mumbled, lifting a shaking hand to her head.

"Yeah, right."

Well, damn, so much for her thinking he was a gentleman. He could at least have pretended not to notice she'd been struck dumb by his looks.

Then she remembered the way he'd swooped down to catch her, how he'd put her on the bed and tenderly taken care of her. She conceded he was definitely a gentleman. Just one with a sense of humor. Considering she'd accused him of being a male prostitute, that was a good thing.

"Am I *really* in your room?"

"I think so," he said. Then he frowned. "Although, to be honest, I could be in the wrong one. My key didn't work, so the bellhop let me in. He didn't speak English very well…maybe we got our wires crossed and he let me into the wrong one."

"Well, if that's the case, feel free to stay."

One brow shot up.

She flushed. "I mean, they can put me in another room. You've already settled in."

"I really don't mind being the one to move. You look like you need to stay right in this bed until tomorrow."

Yeah, and she couldn't deny she wouldn't mind if he stayed in it with her. Well, she couldn't deny it to herself, anyway. She'd deny it to her last breath if he accused her of feeling that way.

"Long trip?"

"You have no idea. I've been traveling for what seems like days."

"From where?"

"Hmm, kind of all over," she said, thinking about the crazy whirlwind her life had become in the past few weeks, ever since she'd become the woman who'd betrayed the beloved Tommy Shane. Whore, slut, bitch, user, taker, Jezebel—some preacher had lobbed that one from a pulpit—those were some of the names that had been launched at her.

So much for thinking she would escape the breakup unscathed. Could she possibly have been more naive? She'd never in a million years imagined that by becoming the bad girl who'd broken the heart of Hollywood's golden boy, she would be loathed, vilified and reviled all over the freaking country.

She'd had paparazzi follow her wherever she went. People who recognized her from her picture on the cover of every tabloid on the newsstand greeted her with catcalls and jeers. Her life had been ripped to shreds on blogs and Hollywood gossip shows. A woman had even spit on her while she was grocery shopping.

So she'd taken off to northern California. Unfortunately, everyone knew she had a twin sister who lived in Napa, and she hadn't been hard to find. Poor Candace and Oliver, who liked to live quietly, had come into the limelight, too.

Then it was off to Florida to visit her parents. Same

story. She hadn't stayed there long. It had been way too much to ask for them to play along when they saw how horribly she was being treated. They knew better than anyone that she and Tommy hadn't had a real engagement, and her father had been dying to defend her. Or at least to punch a few photographers. Heaven forbid she be the cause of his next heart attack!

So distraught over the whole thing that he'd decided to come out, Tommy had planned a press conference. Madison had told him to forget it. What he needed to do was buy her a ticket to somewhere warm. Before long, she was headed for the airport again.

Costa Rica. It should be far enough away for her to regain her sanity. Lord, did she hope so. If this scandal hadn't blown over by the time she went home, she didn't know what she would do.

"Hello?"

She realized her mind had drifted. She cleared her throat. "What?"

"Where'd you go?"

"Nowhere I want to return to," she insisted vehemently.

"You're on the run, huh?"

"You might say that." Something prompted her to add, "You, too?"

He nodded. "Yeah, I guess I am."

"Not a bank robber, are you?" she asked, her tone light and teasing, even though the possibility that he was an ax murderer had flashed across her mind. Of course, if he'd wanted to chop her into kindling, he could easily have done it while she was unconscious. Besides, nobody with eyes as warm and kind as this man's could ever be the violent sort. He looked and behaved like a real-life hero.

"No. I stick strictly to convenience and liquor stores for my life of crime."

"Penny ante," she said with an airy wave of her hand.

"What about you? Are you a secret double agent seducing your way into state secrets?"

She batted her lashes. "You think I could?"

"Honey, I *know* you could."

The vehemence in his tone made her smile fade a bit. They were no longer teasing and joking. The attraction between them had been thick from the moment he'd turned around and found her in his room, but they'd been successfully hiding from it. Except, she suddenly remembered, for that long, heated moment when he'd held her in his arms after he'd caught her. She wasn't a mind reader, but she'd had no difficulty seeing what was going through his head. Probably because the same wild, erotic thoughts had been going through hers.

Sex with a stranger. Nameless, guiltless, hedonistic. Wild and unforgettable and something never to be regretted.

Oh, yes. She'd definitely been thinking those thoughts.

The fact that he had, too, and that he hadn't taken advantage of the situation, reinforced her *hero* assessment. She couldn't think of him as merely a nice guy… that didn't do justice to this man. She barely knew him, yet she knew he was ever so much more than that.

As if he'd noticed the warm, approving way she was

looking at him, he cleared his throat and slid off the bed, standing beside it. "Think you can sit up?"

She nodded, knowing she could do it on her own but somehow unable to refuse his help when he bent and slid a powerful arm behind her shoulders. He helped her into a sitting position and it was all she could do not to turn her head and nip at the rigid muscle flexing near her cheek, or to breathe deeply to inhale his musky, masculine scent.

Tommy had obviously been right. She needed sex, badly. And for a moment, she found herself wishing her first impression had been correct and the man had been for hire. Because completely unencumbered, drop-your-pants-right-now-and-make-me-come sex sounded pretty damned awesome right now.

"By the way," he said as he stepped away from the bed, "I'm Leo. Leo Santori. What's your name?"

"My name?" Considering how desperately she'd been trying to evade the scandal her name created lately, she had to think for a second about how to respond.

"You have one, don't you? It's the thing they give you at the hospital before you get to go home."

"I thought that was a blanket."

"I don't think they give you the blankets anymore."

"Pacifier?"

"Judging by the number of kids my cousins have had, I'm thinking they pretty much ship you out the door with just a red-faced mutant and a big old bill."

She snickered, liking the good humor in his tone. Then she seized on the rest of his comment. "So you don't have any of your own?"

"Pacifiers?"

She smirked. "Kids."

"Nope." He hesitated the briefest moment before adding, "And there's no one waiting in the wings to supply any."

So, he was single? How interesting that he'd felt the need to point that out. How fascinating that the knowledge made her heart leap in her chest.

"What about you?"

"No pacifiers. No kids. Nobody trying to get me to have them."

"Well, that covers just about everything," he said. "Except one… Are you going to tell me your name?"

"It's Madison," she said.

She didn't add the last name. No need to tempt fate, right? He didn't look like the kind of guy who followed Hollywood gossip. Nor did he seem the type who would sell her out to the tabloids. But then, the host of that syndicated radio show hadn't seemed like the type who would release her private number on the air so she could be bombarded with hateful calls and texts, either.

If this Leo Santori was the curious type, he could get online—she supposed even this reclusive resort had internet access—and check her out on Google. If he had her first and last names, he'd come up with a ton of hits, none of which put her in a very good light. Any of them would probably tip somebody off that they could make a quick buck selling her out to the tabloids. That was one reason she'd chosen this resort—they apparently catered to wealthy clientele looking for privacy.

Which made her wonder just what Leo Santori did for a living, and what he'd come here to escape.

"Okay, Madison, how about you stay here? I'll go talk to the people at the front desk and try to get this straightened out. And I'll bring you something to eat when I come back."

"I couldn't…"

"Sure you could. Feel free to dive into the pool and cool off while I'm gone. You look like you could use it."

She glanced out the door, seeing the beautiful swimming pool, so secluded in a private, idyllic garden, and realized he was right. Gliding through that cool water sounded like heaven right now.

"You're sure you don't mind?" she asked, feeling badly but also really not wanting to make that long trudge back to the front desk again.

"I'm sure," he said, heading into the bathroom. The bed was angled so that she had a clear view of him standing in front of the large mirror, and she watched as he grabbed a shirt and pulled it on over his massive shoulders.

Gracious, the man's muscles had muscles. Her heart was being all spastic, thudding and skipping along, and she couldn't seem to even out her breaths to get the right amount of oxygen. She felt light-headed, no longer queasy but there were definitely butterflies fluttering around in her stomach. Her legs were quivering a little, and she was hot between them.

The stranger was totally turning her on, like she couldn't ever remember being turned on before. He was like a miracle worker, a sex god who got women all hot and bothered for a living…except he apparently didn't follow through.

Right. Not a gigolo. Check.

Which was too bad.

You're being ridiculous a little voice in her head said. One thing Madison had never been accused of was having a limited imagination. Considering she wrote stories for a living—one of which was an extremely erotic film that would surely earn an NC-17 rating if it ever got made, and that looked pretty iffy right now—she couldn't deny she'd been thinking about wild, wicked sex a lot lately. It seemed the longer it had been since she'd had it, the more it filled her thoughts.

So much for coming to a secret hideaway to get some peace and tranquillity. If this guy's room was anywhere near hers, she would probably turn into some female Peeping Tom before the week was out. Because her mind just wasn't going to stop thinking about that white towel until she knew what was under it.

"What do you do, anyway?" she asked when he returned, carrying his shoes. *Stripper? Male model?*

"I'm a firefighter."

Her jaw fell open, then she snapped it closed. Because, that totally made sense. She could easily picture him carrying ladders and big, thick hoses. He probably carried one around with him all the time.

Stop it. You're delirious.

"A real American hero?" she said, amused that her instant assessment of him was so dead-on. He really *was* a hero.

"I wouldn't say that," he insisted with a self-deprecating shrug.

"Have you ever saved anyone's life?"

Another shrug. He looked embarrassed. "I guess."

"That was a pretty vague answer to a yes-or-no question," she said, her voice wry. "'I guess' is the type of answer you'd give if someone asked you if you had a good time at a party or if you liked a movie. Saving someone's life seems to require a bit more specificity."

"Okay."

"Was that a yes?"

He grinned. "I guess."

She couldn't help chuckling. "Where do you live?"

"Chicago. You?"

Hmm. Good question. She'd been raised in Florida. Then she'd moved to New York after grad school, determined to be a world-class journalist. Only, she'd realized she kind of hated journalists. That was when she'd started writing screenplays. And when she'd gotten engaged to Tommy, she'd moved to Southern California. Now, she honestly didn't know where she was going to live.

"I'm sort of between housing right now."

That dimple reappeared. "That was a pretty vague answer."

"I suppose it was. I've been living in L.A. But I'm not sure what I'm going to do when I leave here. I might go back to New York."

"Chicago's got better pizza."

Her jaw dropped. "You must be kidding. That loaf of bread with cheese on it that they serve in Chicago has got nothing on a thin, crispy slice of pepperoni from Ray's."

He drew up, looking offended. "My uncle and cousin run a pizza place with food that would make your taste buds decide to commit suicide rather than eat pizza anywhere else ever again."

"With all due respect to your uncle and cousin, you're mental cheese has obviously slipped off its crust. Because you're crazy."

"I challenge you to a taste test."

"I don't think we're going to find very good examples of New York *or* Chicago style here in Central America."

"When we get back stateside then."

Implying they might see each other again after they left here? Oh, how tempting a thought. But she forced herself to concede, an impossible one.

"Maybe," she murmured, quickly looking away. A sharp stab of disappointment shot through her because she knew she was lying.

She couldn't see him again. Not at home. Not here. Once he got the room situation straightened out, she needed to avoid him altogether.

Maybe if he'd been the gigolo she'd thought him, she'd take a chance. Or if he'd been anything but the delightful, warm, friendly, protective man she'd already seen him to be. As it was, though, she couldn't get involved with anybody like Leo Santori. Her life was too freaking messed up right now to involve anyone else in it.

"Well, guess I'll head up to the lobby," he said, as if

noticing that she'd pulled away, if only mentally. "And I was serious, feel free to use the pool."

She nodded. "I might do that. Thanks. Maybe you should take my room key, just in case I'm outside and don't hear you knock."

He picked it up off the dresser where she'd tossed it and departed. After he'd gone, Madison thought about his offer to use the pool. She had been serious about how appealing it sounded, though she wouldn't swim the way she suspected he'd been about to. Judging by the towel he'd been oh-so-inconveniently holding, he'd been planning to skinny-dip. That sounded perfect, delightful, in fact. Letting her naked body soak up the breezes and the warmth was just about her idea of heaven.

Of course, she wasn't quite desperate enough to strip out of her clothes and pose in front of the door the way he had. Even if she did have a very nice ass, if she did say so herself. Still, she wasn't about to bare it for some stranger…a stranger she'd already decided she couldn't have, no matter how much she might want him.

Now that he was gone, now that the room wasn't full of his warm, masculine presence, she managed to pull the rest of her brain cells together. It wasn't just that she couldn't trust anyone she met to keep her secret; there was more to it than that. Coming here to Costa Rica had been about hiding out, licking her wounds, staying out of the limelight and being completely on her own. She needed to rediscover the Madison she'd been six months ago, before her crazy engagement, before she'd become chum for an ocean of avaricious sharks.

There was more, though. She just couldn't do that to *him*...or to any man. Because, even if she could keep him in the dark about who she really was—and the scandal she'd hopefully left behind in the states—she'd be exposing him to a lot of danger, too. The last thing she needed was to get involved with some guy, then get tracked down by the paparazzi. Any man she spent time with would be subject to the same vicious scrutiny she'd endured, maybe even accused of being the mystery lover she'd cheated on Tommy with. The one who didn't exist.

She just couldn't put anybody else through that, especially not someone as great as Leo seemed to be. So, no. There was no room in her life for a fling with a hot fireman. None whatsoever.

Even if she desperately wished there were.

4

As IT TURNED OUT, they'd both been wrong…and right. They were both in the correct room. Apparently, the woman who'd been at the front desk when Leo checked in was the only one who knew how to operate the hotel's computerized system. She'd put Leo in the correct room, even though his key card hadn't been coded properly. Then she'd gone on break, leaving a less-than-capable replacement at the desk. That man had put Madison in Leo's room, too.

Leo couldn't deny that it might be interesting—or, hell, fantastic—to share a bed with the beautiful brunette, but it seemed a bit soon to ask her if she wanted to become roomies.

Maybe by the end of the week…

He'd told the clerk that Madison could keep the room and he'd been assigned to another one. The woman got a twinkle in her eye and offered him a slight brow wag when she noted that Madison was traveling alone, too. Maybe she'd also heard from the bellhop that Madison was young and gorgeous.

Yeesh. He wondered if the clerk had been born a matchmaker or if it merely came with the territory when women reached a certain age. Lord knew there were a lot of them in his family. Of course, even his youngest female cousins seemed to have the gene, so he supposed aging had nothing to do with it.

Heading back to fill Madison in, he couldn't stop himself from thinking about her with every step he took across the grounds.

Madison Reid. She hadn't supplied the last name, the front desk clerk had. He liked it. Liked the woman to whom it was attached, even though he had only just met her.

Leo wasn't a huge believer in fate, but he couldn't deny that this afternoon's incident—them both getting assigned the same room, her walking in on him, him being there to catch her when she fell—seemed pretty out of the ordinary. Like it was meant to happen or something.

He'd come here to enjoy himself, as well as to put the final touches on the coat of I'm-totally-over-Ashley paint he'd been wearing for six months. Truth was, ever since Madison Reid had walked in on him, he hadn't given his former fiancée a moment's thought. And now, as her name crossed his mind, there was only the vaguest sense of recollection, like when he ran into someone he'd gone to elementary school with and couldn't for the life of him come up with their name. He could barely remember what Ashley looked like, or why he'd ever thought he could be happy spending his life with her in the first place.

She'd been beautiful, yes. And pretty successful. But there had been a shallowness to her, not to mention a thin vein of hardness that he'd spotted from the start but had fooled himself into thinking was an indication of strength. Maybe he'd had it all wrong. Maybe the coldness had been a symptom of her weakness, her need to constantly make sure she was the most desired, the most loved woman in the room. Perhaps that was why she'd set out to prove it by getting involved in an affair with his friend. Hell, for all Leo knew, it hadn't been her first.

Funny how easy it was to see her—to understand her—now that the blinders had been so completely torn off his eyes.

Arriving back at his—no, *Madison's*—room, he thrust all those thoughts away. He didn't want to think about his ex now. Not when there were so many other good things to think about.

Lifting a hand, he rapped on the door. No answer. Hoping she'd gone ahead and taken a dip, he inserted her key card and pushed the door open a few inches, calling, "Madison?"

Again, nothing. So he went inside. She wasn't on the bed, and as he crossed the room, he heard a faint splash. Stepping over to the patio slider, which stood open, he glanced outdoors and spotted a dash of red in the clear blue waters of the pool.

A red bikini. God help him.

She was floating on her back, her eyes closed, her arms out to her sides. Her face was turned to the sun and a satisfied smile tugged at those lips. He thought he heard her humming a soft melody.

Madison had been incredibly hot in a skirt and blouse. Now that she'd donned a couple of triangles of scarlet fabric, leaving much of her body bare for his perusal, he could honestly say he'd never seen a sexier female.

Her legs were long—heavenly—and she gently kicked them to keep herself afloat. As he'd noted when she wore the skirt, she had some seriously lush hips, covered only by little sling ties that held her bathing suit together. Those feminine hips were made even more noticeable by the slim waist, flat belly and taut midriff. Her bathing suit top managed to cover only the most essential parts of her full breasts, pushing up those amazing curves, leaving a deep V of cleavage that glistened with droplets of pool water.

All of her glistened. Every inch of that smooth skin, from her pink-tipped toenails on up to her cheeks, on which those long lashes rested, gleamed invitingly. Her thick hair had spread out, floating around her face like a halo, and she looked totally lost to everything but physical sensation as she soaked up the sun and the water.

A sharp, almost painful wave of lust washed over him. His heart thudded, his mouth went dry with a need for moisture only she could provide. His hands fisted at his sides as he tried to push away the images of touching her, stroking her, gliding his fingers along every ridge and valley of her body.

"Oh, you're back!"

He flinched, not having even realized she'd opened her eyes. "Yes. Sorry."

She quickly dropped her legs, standing up in the pool, which was only five feet deep at the most, and smiled up at him. "You were right, this was exactly what I needed. I feel tons better."

"You look better," he admitted through a tight throat. God, he hoped the sun was glaring in her eyes and she couldn't see how taut his entire body was as he tried to keep himself from reacting to her. If she were a couple of feet higher, she'd be eye level with his crotch and would undoubtedly notice the ridge in his jeans. He was hard for the woman, wanting her desperately. Hell, he'd been half-hard for her from the minute he'd caught her in his arms.

"How did everything go with the front desk?"

"All settled. You get the house, I get the kids."

She giggled. The sound was light and sweet, and he liked the tiny laugh lines that appeared beside her eyes. "What kind of mother does that make me?"

"I guess I'm just more soft and nurturing."

Her laughter deepened. "Yeah, you look about as soft as a tree trunk."

Oh, if only she knew.

"What really happened?"

He filled her in on the situation. She didn't seem surprised to hear the guy who'd checked her in had messed things up. But she didn't get all ticked off about it, either. She was calm, chill. He doubted much fazed her... except naked guys catching her when she fell.

He needed to forget about holding her while he was

naked. That was not going to do his pants situation any good at all.

"I brought you back some fruit." The lobby had a large bowl of it available for their guests. It should be enough to settle Madison's stomach until she had a chance to sit down for a real meal.

"Thank you."

"I guess I'll grab my stuff and go. I'm in the Scarlet Room," he told her.

"Maybe the guy at the front desk is color-blind and that's how our wires got crossed. This is the Emerald one, isn't it?"

Grinning, he said, "Yeah, I'm sure that's it."

"Scarlet, huh?" She wagged her brows. "Sounds fit for a sinner."

"Huh, and a little while ago you thought I was a hero."

"I still think that," she said, the teasing note fading from her voice. "I really appreciate you, uh… Where do I start?"

"Flashing you?"

Her sultry laugh heated him more than the late-afternoon sun. "I was going to say catching me, putting me on the bed, putting water on my face, going down to the desk…"

"Not the flashing?"

"I think I fainted before I saw anything."

"You think?"

She gave him a mysterious, half-sideways look. "I'll never tell."

"Thanks for being a gentleman."

"An interesting description for a female."

"I don't know, it just seemed appropriate." Not that anybody would ever mistake her for anything but a pure, sexy woman. "I guess I'll see you later."

She hesitated, her mouth opening, then closing, and then slowly nodded. "Sure. Of course. I'll bet you're tired after your trip."

"Not as tired as you were after yours."

"I really am feeling better." She licked her lips, and furrowed her brow, as if considering something, then added, "I do owe you one for all you've done. How about I buy you a drink sometime this week?"

"I got the all-inclusive package," he said, wondering if she saw the twinkle of pleasure in his eyes.

"So you buy me a drink."

"I could," he said with a bark of laughter, "considering I paid for two packages."

She tilted her head in confusion. Mentally kicking himself for bringing up a subject he really didn't want to discuss, he edged back into her room. "Meet me by the main pool or the beach bar tomorrow and I'll buy you that drink."

"And then you'll tell me why you should be drinking for two?"

"Maybe I will."

"Sorry, that was pushy. You really don't have to."

"Well, then, maybe I won't."

"Touché," she said. "See you later, Leo Santori."

"Bye, Madison Reid."

Her smile faded a little. "How did you know my…"

"Your last name? They mentioned it at the desk."

Realizing she was truly upset about that, he couldn't help wondering why. Was she *really* in hiding? Incognito? He had thought from the moment he saw her that she looked familiar, but had been telling himself it was because she looked like the woman he would dream about if he wanted to have the best, most erotic dreams of his life. But maybe it was more than that.

"Are you famous?"

"Maybe infamous," she mumbled under her breath.

He quirked a curious brow. She didn't elaborate. A long silence stretched between them, and he realized she didn't intend to.

Hmm. Interesting.

But he wasn't here to dig into anybody else's secrets. He'd just wanted to get away from his own drama. No responsibilities, no angst, no worrying about a broken engagement or the fact that his family was apprehensive about him and his friends were insisting he get out there and get laid as some kind of get-back-at-his-ex game.

He wasn't into any of that. Coming here to Costa Rica was about leaving everything else behind and just indulging in some sun, some fun and some pleasure.

And now that he'd met Madison, he began to suspect things were going to be even more sunny, fun and pleasurable than he had anticipated.

BY THE TIME she awoke the next morning, having slept a solid, uninterrupted nine hours—largely because of the fresh air blowing in on her through the screen door all night long, not to mention the utter exhaustion—

Madison woke up the next day a little unsure of what to do with herself.

She'd never been on a vacation alone, though she'd been on plenty of family trips as a kid, of course. And she, Candace and Tommy had gone away together several times, usually on college road trips to dive-places on the beach. There'd also been one skiing trip with a boyfriend. But never had she been in a foreign land all by herself, with nowhere to go, no one to see, nothing to do and no schedule to keep.

All she had to do was stay hidden from the press.

She couldn't help wondering what was going on back in California. She hadn't spoken with Tommy or with Candace since she'd left Florida, although she imagined they'd both tried to reach her. She'd bet there were messages on her cell phone and texts and emails. They'd been so worried about her, for once both of them thinking they had to be the protectors, the caretakers. She suspected they were constantly on the phone with each other, trying to figure out what to do.

Though he'd lived with Madison for the past six months, in some ways, Tommy still seemed closer to Candace. Madison was never envious of that, however, knowing their friendship was very different. With creative, artistic, kindhearted Candace, Tommy could be carefree and a little more whimsical. With Madison—much more no-nonsense and blunt than her twin—he had to man up and take responsibility for what he did. And of course, with him, both the Reid twins could be more daring and adventurous.

As far as she was concerned, the three of them brought out the absolute best in each other.

Four. There are four of us now.

Right. Because Candace—her other half—had gotten herself a *new* other half in the form of a hunky lawyer who'd posed as a gardener and planted baskets of love in Candy's heart. Blech.

Madison liked Oliver. She really did. But she still wasn't sure she would ever get over the feeling that she'd lost something vital when she'd become the second most important person in her twin's life.

It's not four, it's five.

Pesky math. But the addition was right. Because Tommy had Simon, and Madison had the feeling he'd be in the picture for a very long time. Meaning she truly was, she realized, the odd man out. Literally the fifth wheel. It was the first time she'd acknowledged it, and a sudden hollowness opened up within her, swallowing some of her happiness and her certainty that nothing could ever really change the relationships she had with those she loved. Things had changed, and continued to change.

She was the only one who hadn't found that mystical connection called love. Honestly, she wasn't sure she ever would. She'd dated men, she'd slept with men, she'd even lived with one before Tommy. But never had she had stars in her eyes the way her sister did, and never had she tap-danced through her day because the right guy smiled at her the way Tommy did.

"Enough, no more feeling sorry for yourself," she muttered as she forced her mind toward other things.

Like what she could do with plenty of money and an exotic, tropical paradise to explore.

There were a lot of things she could do, and someone with whom she'd really like to do them. But having fallen asleep last night thinking of all the reasons that being with Leo Santori would be a really bad idea, she had pretty well decided not to do them. Or, to do them alone.

Zip lining, ecotouring, bodysurfing…they could all be done alone, or with a professional instructor. But the thing she most wanted to do wouldn't be nearly as fun without Leo.

Ah, well. It wouldn't be the first time she'd had sex alone, that was for sure. Lately it was all she'd had.

Of course, she hadn't exactly tucked any sex toys into her luggage. She wondered how often Customs asked travelers to turn on those odd-looking devices, and was glad she hadn't had to find out. But the point was, she was left totally on her own when it came to dealing with the intense, er, *interest* Leo had aroused in her from the moment she'd first seen him.

Oh, yeah, that picture had been burned in her brain.

Madison had always had an active imagination, and had never needed erotic stories or movies to rev her engines. Lately, just thinking about the hero of the screenplay she'd written was enough to get her going. The dark, angry, possibly murderous antihero liked his sex rough and dangerous, with floggers and leather ropes and lots of "Yes, sirs."

While she'd been writing it, that had been her fantasy: being tied up, forced to be submissive, learning how pain could be pleasurable. Well, maybe not her fantasy, but she'd certainly wondered about it, digging into a deep, previously untapped part of herself to create those scenes that disturbed more than titillated.

But now, with Leo's incredibly handsome face and warm, gentle eyes in her mind, she could only think of long, slow, sexy loving that went on for hours and needed no props, just two slick, aroused bodies bathed in sunshine and warm air. No touch off-limits, no sensation forbidden, every eroticism imbued with gentleness and intimacy. And trust. Lots of trust.

She moaned a little, and began to touch all the places on her body that would have far preferred his hands to hers. Running her fingers over her breast, she plumped it, knowing his big hands would overflow if he were to cup them. She reached for her nipple—hard and filled with sensation. Plucking it, teasing it, she acknowledged that she would never really have lived if that man never sucked her nipples.

She whimpered, one hand gliding even farther, over her hip, and then her belly. Farther. She brushed her index finger through the tiny thatch of hair—the landing strip look that was so popular in Southern California. Madison had gone for it once she'd moved out there, but hadn't had a lover since she'd first begun waxing her pubis, and had wondered, more than once, what it would feel like to have a man's mouth on that bare, sensitive skin. Her own fingers felt divine, made slick and smooth by her body's moisture. She moved them slowly, gently, stroking herself just right. Her clit was hard and ever so sensitive, and she made tiny circles around it, drawing out the pleasure, picturing his hands, his tongue.

Another stroke. She gasped, arching her back, curling her toes. Her climax washed over her, quick, hard and hot, and she sprawled out in the bed, trying to even her breaths and calm down.

It didn't happen. For the first time in her life, masturbating hadn't taken the edge off. Yes, she'd had an orgasm, but it hadn't satisfied her. She was still edgy, swollen and in need, as if she'd been cut off in the middle of intensely pleasurable foreplay.

It wasn't hard to figure out why. She wanted a man. One man. Leo. Her own hands just weren't going to cut it. She wanted him to be the one to make her come, wanted his cock inside her when he did it.

She'd told herself all last evening during her room service meal and the long minutes she'd thought about him before drifting off to sleep that she couldn't have him. Couldn't allow herself to take him. But never had she *really* acknowledged what that meant. Or how incredibly difficult it would be to stick by that decision. Because if she couldn't release this tension, she was going to lose her mind. And the only man who could release it for her was one she'd already decided was off-limits. He was too nice, too good, too heroic. Definitely not somebody who deserved to be tarnished with the scandal surrounding her.

"Damn it," she muttered. "Why did you have to go

and be so wonderful?" If he'd been a jerk or a player, it would have been much easier to let go of her concerns and *take* what she wanted.

There was, of course, no answer. Nothing could possibly explain why she'd met a man so sexy, so delicious, so freaking adorable, now, when she was in no position to have him.

Knowing she couldn't stay in bed and continue to be sexually frustrated, she got up and tried to decide between a shower and a morning swim. She intended to go down to the open-air restaurant for breakfast. From the hotel information sheet, she'd noticed that it adjoined the large resort pool. She planned to lie out beside it, so there wasn't much point in showering first, especially since she'd taken one last night before bed.

But she certainly wouldn't be able to swim naked in the public pool, and right now, swimming naked— letting cool water comfort and soothe her overly sensitized private parts—sounded like the perfect cure for what ailed her.

She'd gone skinny-dipping before; what adventurous, Florida-raised kid hadn't? But she'd certainly never done it in broad daylight. Considering the privacy of her pool, though, she figured she could risk it. Leo certainly had been about to yesterday. Good for the goose and all that.

Decision made, she got up and went into the bathroom to brush her teeth. She scooped her hair back into a ponytail, and grabbed the towel she'd used the afternoon before. The one that still carried the faintest scent of the man who'd been holding it when she'd entered her room.

Yeah, using Leo's towel had been pretty pathetic. It had also been pretty delightful, rubbing it against her cool body, smelling him, remembering him.

"Stop it," she ordered herself, determined to put the man out of her mind for the rest of the day. Hell, for the rest of her trip!

Going to the screen door, she pulled it open and stuck her head outside, peeking around. It felt so strange to step out into broad daylight—God, what a gorgeous, clear, sunny morning it was—not wearing a stitch. She caught her bottom lip between her teeth, glancing back and forth from one side of the walled-hedged area to the other. The tangle of green shrub was thick and practically impossible to see through. Plate-size pink flowers helped, too.

"Just do it. Just jump in!" she ordered herself.

So she did. She dropped the towel and wound her way around the lounge chairs that stood under the covered awning right outside the door. Free, excited and naked, she plowed forward, not thinking, just striding the five steps to the pool and taking a leap of faith.

It should have taken a few seconds for her to hit the water.

It didn't. It took forever, considering time had stopped.

She moved in slow motion, horror washing over her.

Because, after her feet had left the concrete deck— after she was committed to the pool and it was too late to change her mind—she saw a dark shape swimming toward her.

A dark, sinuous shape that hit on every one of her most elemental fears and sent hysteria coursing through her body.

There was nothing else to do. She screamed bloody murder.

5

THE ROOM SERVICE breakfast Leo had ordered lived up
to the hotel's reputation for outstanding food. He'd enjoyed every bite of his meal, which he'd consumed outside on his patio, having moved his café table and chairs
outdoors. It was midmorning, the sun was shining, the
breeze was blowing, and he was on vacation. Life didn't
get much better than this, especially when he thought
about the chilly autumn and frigid winter that awaited
him when he returned to Chicago.

He had made some plans for his first full day in
Costa Rica, starting with dropping by his next-door
neighbor's room.

He hadn't been able to put Madison out of his mind
since he'd left her yesterday afternoon. Especially not
once he'd realized the Scarlet Bungalow—his suite—
was the very next one down the path from hers. Their
private courtyards butted up against one another and
he'd heard her humming again as she'd floated the pre-
vious afternoon. He'd stayed quiet, not wanting to dis-

turb her, somehow knowing they could use a bit of a time before they saw each other again.

She needed some sleep, some food and some energy. He needed to think about what he was going to do about the incredible attraction he felt for the woman.

Today he'd knock on her door and see where things went.

He'd just finished off the last bite of his toast and reached for his coffee cup, sweetened with raw sugar and thick cream, when the morning silence was pierced by a dramatic, shrill scream.

He flinched, nearly dropping his cup, and was on his feet before he'd made up his mind to get out of his chair. His whole body went on instant alert, like it did whenever the alarm sounded at the station house, not knowing if he would be dousing a small oven fire or battling a monster blaze in an abandoned warehouse.

The scream had been cut off sharply—as if the screamer had run out of breath—and that made things even worse. Because he feared he knew where it had come from.

His stomach churned.

"Madison!" he said, knowing the woman's cry of terror had come from the other side of the hedged wall surrounding his pool.

Not giving it another thought, he ran over to the hedge, shoved his hands into the thick greenery and gripped the cool stone wall behind it. He clambered up, his bare feet and legs getting scratched, his arms covered with sticky green moisture, his face slapped with flowers. He lost his footing once, skidded down a few inches, then gripped the top even more tightly in his hand so he wouldn't go tumbling back down.

As he reached the top of the six-foot-tall wall, he heard splashes and another shriek. Was she being attacked? Drowning?

His heart raced. "I'm coming!" he called as he launched over the top of the wall, flinging himself into her private courtyard. He landed on his feet in the mulch, right beside her privacy hedge, and immediately looked for her. Having heard the splashes, his eyes turned right to the pool.

Madison was in it, her face twisted with fear, her mouth open as she exhaled shallow gasps. She didn't even appear to see him. All her attention was focused on the water before her. She was struggling to back up to the rear edge of the pool, reaching behind her, waving her arms, as if afraid to turn and look for it. Afraid to tear her attention off whatever had grabbed it.

"Madison, what is it?"

Her lips trembled. She cast the tiniest glance in his direction. But she didn't have to answer. He suddenly saw for himself.

"Stay still, don't move," he snapped, seeing the creature swimming in the shallow end of the pool.

A snake. Not huge, but big enough—thick, though not terribly long. Boa constrictor, if he had to guess, though he was no expert.

Jesus, no wonder she was screaming like somebody had come at her with an ax. He might have, too. He liked snakes about as much as Indiana Jones did.

But he needed to keep her calm. If she started flailing around, the thing might notice her and come closer to investigate. And while he would never let it get near her, his Tarzan-snake-wrestling skills were a wee bit rusty. Or nonexistent.

"It's okay," he told her, trying to keep her calm with his voice as he edged along the side of the pool. "He's not going to bother you."

"Snake. Oh, God, a snake. I hate snakes, Leo," she said, whimpering.

"I'm not a big fan either, darlin', but I don't think he's paying too much attention to you. He just wanted to take a swim."

"Aren't there j-jungles, rivers, entire oceans?" she said, panic rising in her voice. "Why my pool? Why now when I'm naked and jumped in without looking!"

His mind tried to make him think about that naked part but he was too focused on the way her voice was shaking and the danger the animal posed to her. If it *was* a boa, it wasn't poisonous, which was a good thing. But he doubted anything he said was going to make her feel better.

"Listen to me now," he said as he spied the pool supply closet tucked up against the corner of her bungalow. Hopefully it would contain a skimmer; he doubted the maintenance men would carry them room to room every day. "I'll take care of it, Madison. But I need you to very *calmly* get to the edge of the pool and climb out."

"I c-can't…"

"Of course you can. I'll watch it so you can turn around."

"No."

"Just move slowly."

"Have you forgotten the naked p-part?" she groaned, though he wasn't sure if her voice was shaking due to fear of the snake or embarrassment over her—*gulp*—nakedness.

"I won't look," he promised.

And he wouldn't. He was focused on the snake and the closet and would not allow himself to cast so much as a glimpse at her lithe form gleaming beneath the water. Not while he still had an unwelcome visitor to contend with.

It was just his luck to catch her skinny-dipping when she was in real physical danger.

He edged sideways, noting there was no lock on the closet and finding himself very thankful for that. Reaching it, he yanked the door open, tore his attention off the snake long enough to assess what was inside and gratefully spotted not only a skimmer on a long pole, but also a sizeable bucket that had once held chemicals but was now empty. A lid lay beside it on the concrete floor of the storage closet.

Looking back to assure her, he realized she had moved closer to the wall but still hadn't taken her eyes off the snake. "Okay, it's time to climb out now, Madison," he told her as he retrieved the items from the closet. "Once I try to grab him, he's going to panic and swim away."

She didn't argue anymore. From the corner of his eye, he saw her do as he'd said and put her hands on the pool's edge. Then his attention zoomed right back to her swimming companion.

He moved to the edge of the pool, placing the bucket

close by and trying to gauge just how quick he'd have to be if he wanted to swoop that sucker up and drop him inside it. Part of him thought about just leaving it, getting her inside and calling the hotel to deal with it. But he knew if he did, she would never have another moment's peace. It could easily slither away and if it did, she'd be envisioning it returning every time she closed her eyes. Hell, his bungalow was right next door…so would he!

"Ready?" he asked, not glancing toward her, though he saw her vague shape standing on the far side of the pool. He had a quick impression of hands crossed in the Eve-old woman's modesty pose, but that was all. "Madison?"

She only groaned.

He took a deep breath, then plunged the skimmer into the water, an inch below the animal, and jerked his arms to lift it out of the pool. It immediately squirmed and almost fell over the side, but luck was with him. He was able to flip it right into the waiting bucket.

The snake immediately began to slither up to escape, but he covered the opening with the skimmer, blocking its exit while he grabbed the lid. Then he switched them, catching the angry animal inside, grabbing a large, decorative rock to place on it so the lid wouldn't pop back off. It had taken no more than thirty seconds, but his heart was racing, and his breaths were choppy and forced, as if he'd just run a block wearing his protective gear and carrying a ladder.

"Oh, my God, thank you, thank you, thank you."

He turned just as Madison threw herself against him,

wrapping her arms around his neck, burying her face in the crook. She shuddered, her entire form quaking.

"It's okay, it's over."

"I hate snakes. I'm terrified of them. When I saw that thing in the pool a second *after* I'd leaped in, I thought I'd have a heart attack and die."

"Well, it's done. I'll call the front office and have them send somebody down to take care of it."

She shivered again. "I can't even look at one of them. I know it's irrational, it's stupid, but I just… I'm *offended* by them, somehow. Does that make any sense?" She pulled back a little and rubbed away some moisture that had appeared in her eyes. "My rational mind understands why snakes are needed for the environment, and I know the chances of ever being bitten by one, much less dying, are slim to none. But they just offend some deep, primal part of me."

He believed her. There was no way he couldn't. Her voice was hoarse, shaking, and her eyes were slightly wild. She looked almost on the verge of hysteria.

He slid his arms around her waist, holding her tightly against him, and stroked his fingertips in the hollow of her back. "It's okay. It's over. Shh."

Her head dropped onto his shoulder, and they stood there for few long moments. He could feel her gasping breaths, not to mention her racing heart thudding against his. He continued to whisper consoling words to her, brushing his lips against her damp hair, then against her temple where the pulse fluttered wildly. He would have thought she would have begun to calm down by now, but if anything her heart seemed to be pounding even harder against his chest.

His bare chest.

Which was pressed against her bare chest.

Which went along with her bare *everything*.

Holy shit. In the excitement, he'd momentarily forgotten what she wasn't wearing. She'd been—and was now—completely naked.

He should let her go, spin around, turn his back and toss her a towel. A nice guy would do that. The hero she'd called him would do that.

Leo didn't do that.

He just couldn't. Not yet. Not when she felt so good—so pliant and womanly. Now, when she was curled up against him like she needed his warmth to revive every cell in her body, how could he possibly step away from her?

He continued to stroke the small of her back, then let one hand glide down to brush against the top curve of her buttock. She sighed against his neck, pressing her lips against his raging pulse, telling him not to stop. Considering stopping hadn't even been on the top ten list of possibilities, that wouldn't be a problem.

Her body was all lush curves and softness, and he loved the texture of her skin beneath his fingers. He continued to stroke the curve of her bottom, tracing a line to her hip, which he cupped in his hand. She was so perfectly shaped, with the indentation of her waist designed to be wrapped in a man's arms, those hips intended to be clung to by someone buried to the hilt inside her.

"Leo," she groaned, kissing his neck again.

Her warm, soft tongue slipped out and tasted his ear-lobe, and he groaned low in his throat.

Her invitation wasn't voiced, but it was clear just the same. He didn't know whether they would have ended up like this if not for her fright. He had no idea whether she'd been tortured by the same kind of long, restless, sleepless night he had, filled with erotic dreams and even more erotic fantasies. He didn't even know if this was going to go anywhere else. All he knew was he had to kiss her.

So he did. Not saying another word, he lifted a hand to her hair, sliding his fingers into the tangled pony-tail, and tugged her head back so she was looking up at him. Giving her face a searching glance, he dropped his mouth onto hers.

Soft at first. A tiny shared breath. Then they both fell into the kiss.

It was easy, so easy. And so good.

Her tongue met his with a languorous thrust, and he drank deeply of her, exploring every bit of her mouth. He found himself wanting to memorize the shape of her, the scent of her, the feel of her. They stroked and licked, tangled, gave and took. She tasted sweet and minty, delicious, and having his mouth pressed against hers felt as natural and right as coming home after a long time away.

His hand still cupped her hip, and he stroked her, held her tightly against him. With his other one, he traced a path up her midriff to the side of a full breast, pressed flat against his chest. He was dying to see her, to let his other senses be filled by her, but right now, memorizing her taste was enough. It had to be enough.

She was groaning, sighing, and her own hands explored, too. She tangled one in his hair, fingering it, twisting it, holding him close as if afraid he might end the kiss before they'd both had their fill.

Her other hand dug into his shoulder before sliding down his arm. Their fingers curled together, then she reached between them to stroke his stomach. Her hand drifted close, so damned close, to his rigid cock, which was so hard, it had pushed up beyond the top of his swim trunks.

"Oh, God," she groaned against his mouth, realizing what had happened as she caressed the swollen tip.

His body was helpless to resist the age-old urge to thrust toward her touch. Those soft, delicate fingers flicked lightly over his skin, the tip of her thumb smoothing out the moisture that seeped from him.

Before he could think or breathe or move, she'd tugged the trunks farther away from his groin, making room for her hand. She slipped it down, rubbing her palm all along the back of his cock, her long nails scraping ever so delicately on his tight balls.

He groaned, again rocking toward her, loving that she responded to his blatant need by wrapping her hand around him, at least as much as she could, and squeezing lightly. He heard her whimper. The sound seemed to convey both excitement and perhaps nervousness, as if she had just figured out, since her fingers couldn't close entirely around him, how much he had to offer her.

She didn't have to be nervous. He could make her

wet enough to take every inch of him. And he was *desperate* to do it. More than he wanted to live until sundown did he want to sink into her—her mouth, her sex, somewhere wet and hot and slippery. And tight. Oh, God, yeah, *tight*.

She stroked him, up and down, matching the movements with each warm thrust of her tongue. He edged away, just enough to slide his fingers over one full breast, until he could tweak the hard nipple between them. She hissed into his mouth as he played with her, stroking her into a series of slow shudders.

She made no sound of resistance at all when he moved his other hand from her hip, back around to her bottom, so he could toy with the seam separating those lush curves. A tiny stroke, another, then she relaxed enough to let him play a little more. She was pliant in his arms, arching a bit in invitation, and he dipped his fingers farther…enough to get wet, to sample the juices of her body, hot and slick and welcoming.

He had time to mentally process the fact that her plump, engorged lips were completely bare—*want, want, want*—when she whimpered. "You— We…"

He didn't know what she was about to say—to ask, to demand. Because before she had a chance to continue, they both heard a thumping sound coming from the ground near their feet.

She obviously realized what it was before he did, because she yanked back and leaped away so fast she almost fell into the pool. Leo got the tiniest glimpse at her utterly gorgeous, naked body—God, those breasts were a thing of art—before he focused his attention on what had made the sound.

Mr. Snake was trying to get out of his container. The lid on the bucket was jiggling up and down, and the whole bucket was a bit wobbly. He pulled his trunks up and retrieved another, heavier rock and replaced the one he'd put on there, being sure to leave uncovered a small hole in the old lid. He didn't like the intruder, but he also wanted to make sure the critter would get enough air during the few minutes it took to get somebody down here to get rid of him.

While he resecured the prisoner, Madison grabbed a towel off the ground and wrapped it around herself, sarong style. By the time he straightened and returned his full attention to her, she was covered from breast to upper thigh. He mourned that he had lost his chance to see that incredible, luscious body he'd felt pressing against him, and he knew there would be no diving back into the crazy-hot kiss they'd been sharing. Much less all the other crazy-hot things they'd been doing…and had planned to do.

"Wow," she whispered, lifting a hand to her mouth. That hand was shaking, those lips were trembling, her voice was quivery. Whether she was more freaked out by the snake or by the embrace, he didn't know, but he sure hoped he had a leg up on the slithery reptile.

"I guess I should apologize," he said, not really sure why. If she hadn't enjoyed that, he'd turn in his membership as a dude.

"For saving my life?"

He rolled his eyes. "I don't think it's poisonous."

"I meant, you saved me from a heart attack. I really don't think you understand how much snakes terrify me."

"I think I have a pretty good idea."

She was already shaking her head in disagreement before he'd finished his sentence. "I'm not just being a wimp. Believe me, I'm not scared of much." She thrust a hand in her hair, knocking the ponytail holder out altogether so that those honey curls bounced around her shoulders in a thick, sexy tangle. "I don't usually go around fainting, and I don't remember another time in my adult life that I have ever screamed with terror. Except, maybe, the first time I went skydiving."

Okay. So she was pretty brave.

"But snakes. Oh, God, snakes. They're my Achilles' heel. My sister, Candace, she can't stand spiders. Me? Hell, a guy I dated had a pet tarantula and I used to walk around with him sitting on my shoulder."

"The guy or the tarantula?"

She punched him lightly on the arm. Frankly, he preferred it when she used that hand to squeeze his cock.

But they'd moved past that moment. It was over… at least for now. Sanity and reality had intruded, and she was going to focus on the snake rather than on the near sex.

Letting her get away with it, knowing she probably needed to regroup and think about what had almost happened, he rubbed his upper arm, as if she'd hurt him, and grinned. "Sorry. I got the point, you're okay with bugs."

"Yeah, no big deal. I'd protect Candace from spiders,

she'd protect me from snakes, and Tommy would protect us both from guys who didn't take no for an answer."

"Tommy? Your brother?"

She opened her mouth, then snapped it shut. Some of the high color began to leave her cheeks, and he watched as she clenched her hands together in front of her.

"No, a friend. Boy next door. We grew up together."

"Okay."

He wondered if that was really all, considering how skittish she'd gotten when she'd mentioned the guy. But it wasn't his place to pry.

"Anyway, I know I have ophidiophobia. It's irrational and I've tried to get over it. I've studied, I even got myself hypnotized once."

One of his brows shot up. "Really?"

"Well, it was at one of those girls' naughty-panty party things, with a bunch of women drinking wine and buying fancy underwear. A friend of one of my college roommates was there and she swore she could hypnotize any of us into losing weight or quitting smoking. So I asked her to try to un-ophidiophobia me."

He was having a hard time paying attention, his mind still back on the whole panty party concept. Jeez, did chicks really do that? And how did one sign up to be a salesperson?

"It didn't work."

"No?"

"When she got me under and told me to visualize a snake curled up peacefully at my feet, I apparently threw up all over the saleslady's panty box."

Oh, did he need her to change this conversation. But

because he was a masochist, he replied, "Guess you bought a lot of underwear that night."

"Yeah, right. You hurl on it, you buy it." She wrapped her arms around herself, clinging to the towel, and continued, "So, you see, it's a big deal to me. I was on the verge of a full-on panic attack, and you saved me, and I appreciated it so much, and that's why I threw myself into your arms. It wasn't… I didn't…"

"I get it. You weren't trying to take advantage of me."

She nibbled her lip. "Right."

"Understood."

"And you're not, uh, mad?"

Oh, sure. Because every dude would be really angry about a beautiful, naked woman throwing her arms around him to express her gratitude. Or half jerking him off until he'd become nothing but nine inches of sensation.

"Not mad. I promise."

She looked relieved.

"Now, how about I go in and call the front desk and ask them to send somebody out here to get rid of our friend."

Her eyes rounded into circles. "I'm not staying out here by myself with that thing! He might tip the bucket over. He could…"

"Come with me then," he said, cutting her off and pulling her into her room. He shut the screen door behind them. "We'll make the call together."

She looked visibly relieved. "Okay. And then you can hand me the phone so I can call the airline. Because

there's no way in hell I'm staying here and risking another run-in with the Creature from the Black Lagoon."

His heart skipped a beat and his stomach turned over.
"You're leaving?"

She blinked, as if finally thinking about the words
she'd said. She glanced at the closed door, shivered, then
looked back at him. "That sounds ridiculous, doesn't
it? I mean, there are snakes everywhere."

"Yes."

"I'm overreacting."

"Just a little."

"The thing is, I really don't know if I could ever
be comfortable walking around the grounds again by
myself."

"I'm sure you could."

"I've never vacationed alone."

"Me, either."

She tapped the tip of her finger on her bottom lip.
"I'm wondering if we could, maybe, vacation alone...
together."

His jaw fell open.

"I mean, it would be nice to know somebody had
your back, wouldn't it?"

"Sure," he said with a nod. "I could totally use somebody to save me from any tarantulas that sneak into
my room."

If he woke up with one of those suckers lying on
top of him, the whole town would hear his screeches.

"And you've proved yourself to be a champion snake
wrangler."

A slow smile tugged at his lips. It was answered by

one from her. Maybe her first real one since he'd heard her scream and ran forward to be her dragon, er, snake, slayer. Well, not slayer—he'd never kill an innocent animal that was just doing what animals did—snake *catcher* would be the better term.

"You asking me if I want to be your vacation buddy?" he finally said.

"Something like that. You know, like in kindergarten when you always had to have a partner to hold hands with in the lunch line."

He grimaced. "I'd never have held hands with a *girl*."

"I don't have cooties."

He grinned and walked closer, lifting a hand to push her hair back over her shoulder. "I can tell."

She stared at him, licked her lips, then edged away, as if confused, a little skittish and shy remembering that heated embrace they'd shared.

Again, he let her get away with it, knowing they'd get back there sooner or later. Right now, she was telling herself, and him, that she was just after a buddy to spend time with and cover her back during her vacation. But he knew deep down it was more than that. The encounter was driving her decisions, even if she hadn't yet realized it. Somewhere deep inside, she wanted more. This was a logical, acceptable way to tell him she wanted to spend time with him.

Of course, shoving her hand down his trunks and grabbing his cock had been a pretty good indication, too. In fact, he preferred it.

"I suppose I could check out your pool every day before you get in it."

She shuddered. "Definitely."

"And come running if you call?"

"How did you manage that, anyway?" she asked, as if finally remembering what had happened before he'd caught the snake. "Where'd you come from? I know my door was locked."

"Over the wall. We're next-door neighbors."

A laugh escaped her lips and for the first time that morning, he began to think she was really going to be all right. Her panic had eased its grip on her and she was regaining her equilibrium.

That was a good thing, even if her cute suggestion—that he be her vacation buddy—was driving him crazy. The idea that he could be buddies with a woman who had every one of his senses, and all of his male chromosomes, on high alert, was ludicrous.

But he knew she was only half-joking. The thought of leaving really had crossed her mind, all because of a run-in with a member of the local population. And he didn't want her to go. He *desperately* didn't want her to go.

So, not even giving it any more thought, he agreed to her suggestion.

"Okay, Madison Reid, you've got yourself a deal."

"I do?"

"Uh-huh. Let's be solo vacationers together."

And see just how long it took for them to progress beyond the holding-hands-in-the-lunch-line stage.

6

THE HOTEL STAFF was incredibly apologetic about the snake incident. After Leo had called the front desk and explained the situation, no fewer than four maintenance men had shown up at her door. They'd deftly taken care of her unwanted visitor, and had then, at Leo's suggestion, looked over every inch of her private courtyard, cutting back some of the lower tangles of hedge to make sure there were no holes, nests or sleeping family members. She had remained inside, unwilling to even look out the door for fear they'd stumble across Mrs. Snake and a passel of little snakelings.

They hadn't. They'd found an indentation under one corner of the wall, where they assumed the wild creature had made its entry, and had backfilled it in with packed dirt and stone. The foreman had gone on to assure her that nothing like this had ever happened before and it most certainly wouldn't happen again.

Right. Just her luck to get the pool with the big honking reptile in it.

Of course, it had also been just her luck to have a big, powerful hunk right next door to save her ass.

Lucky me.

Good Lord, was he big and powerful. Even now, a couple of hours later, she couldn't stop thinking about how his body had felt pressed against hers, so strong and masculine. Not to mention how he'd tasted. How he'd smelled.

How that massive ridge of heat had swelled between them during their passionate kiss, making her legs grow weak and her mouth as dry as straw.

She'd thrown her naked self into his arms, not even pausing to think of how he might react. And he'd reacted. Oh, had he ever. She knew for a fact she'd never been with a man who'd *reacted* more. Or had more to react *with.* Wrapping her hand around him the way she had had taken a lot of gall, and she knew it. But she hadn't cared. She still didn't. She'd wanted to touch him and had been desperate for him to touch her.

No, she wouldn't regret this morning. Not ever.

Unless, of course, it was never repeated.

Then she might regret it, because she would be left wondering just how amazing all the *other* things they could have done together would be.

She lifted her hand and fanned it in front of her face, needing it more for her heated imagination than the warm weather. As they lay on a pair of huge, padded lounge chairs beside the stunning tropical pool that dominated the center of the resort grounds, she found herself continuing to cast glances toward his swim trunks, wondering if the lumps in the fabric were caused by the looseness of the material, or by the fact that he was still half-aroused. As she was, even hours later.

She gulped and forced herself to focus on the book she'd brought along, not wanting to distract herself all over again by remembering how wonderful it had felt to be in his arms. And how wonderful it would be to be in his bed.

That was where they were heading. She could no longer deny it to herself. The attraction was too strong, irresistible, and now that they'd kissed, touched each other, she knew there was only one place this kind of want could take them.

He had to have figured that out, too. But for now, he seemed content to be her "buddy." He'd insisted on escorting her down to the pool, making a big production of showing her how carefully he was inspecting the path in front of them. She'd finally begun to laugh and admitted she might have overreacted just a bit, and had found that laughing with Leo was almost as delightful as kissing him.

"What do you suppose is this surprise the hotel is planning for us?" Leo asked, startling her. She'd thought he was sleeping—his eyes were concealed by dark sunglasses, and he'd been lying quietly for several minutes, which had enabled her to, she thought, sneakily glance at him and wonder how on earth his skin could stretch enough to accommodate all those muscles.

"I'm not sure." Madison reached for her drink— a tall, fruity concoction laced with rum that the bartender kept sending over. Apparently, word had gotten out about her close encounter with nature, and the hotel was bending over backward to make it up to them. "I've been wondering about it, too. Whatever it is, it sounds like it's going to be pretty special."

Not only had she been upgraded to a completely all-inclusive vacation, meaning she wouldn't have to pay for any more meals or drinks, she and Leo had also been invited to a private surprise dinner that evening. The hotel was making all the arrangements and kept insisting it was the very least they could do for the inconvenience.

Personally, she preferred they give her a pair of snakeskin boots, but she supposed that was being a little vindictive and bloodthirsty. She wasn't a subscriber to the adage "the only good snake is a dead snake." She simply didn't ever want to have to see, hear or interact with one again as long as she lived.

"I guess they take their snake incursions seriously," she said.

"I suppose it wouldn't do their hotel any good if word got out that their pools came complete with their own boa constrictors."

She shuddered, hating to even think about it. That thing had been a boa, one of the maintenance men had confirmed it. He'd also said it was extremely rare for them to come out of the jungle, but that they did sometimes enjoy taking a freshwater dip. Again, just her luck. Maybe she had a sign on her back that she couldn't see, saying Fuck with me.

"I'm surprised they didn't just offer you a spa day or something," Leo said. "No need to include me."

"Hey, you were the snake catcher. I just stood there naked and screamed."

He smiled broadly. "Yeah. I remember."

She leaned over and flicked his arm sharply. He just laughed.

"Of course, I have a feeling that the woman at the front desk is doing a little matchmaking," he said.

She gaped. "Seriously?"

"Uh-huh. I wouldn't be at all surprised if this turns out to be some romantic setup."

Hmm. That didn't sound so bad.

"Though, they didn't make it sound like we had to dress up or anything," he said, "which is a good thing since I didn't bring much more than jeans and trunks."

"Me, either."

"So you weren't planning on doing any clubbing or hobnobbing while you were here, huh?"

She snorted. "Definitely not. I planned to do exactly what I'm doing right now."

She just hadn't planned to do it with a hunky firefighter from Chicago.

"So why did you decide to take a solo vacation?" he asked, sounding a little puzzled, as if he'd been thinking about it since she'd mentioned this morning that they were both vacationing alone.

She tensed, but didn't overreact. It was a natural question. Everywhere around them were groups and couples. The airport had been full of them, as had the taxi line. And even here, at such a small hotel, one only saw pairs walking about. Right now, on the other side of the lagoon-shaped, flower-bedecked pool, she saw two cooing couples, one middle-aged, another young and honeymoonish. This wasn't the type of place one vacationed alone.

"I was going through some stuff and just needed to get out of town alone for a while." She shrugged. "As it turns out, it might be a great thing."

He smiled lazily.

"Because now I can finish up a project I'm working on," she said a little teasingly, knowing he'd thought she was referring to him. She had been. But that had sounded a little too fawning.

Besides, now that she'd voiced it, she had to admit, the project idea wasn't a bad one. She might be persona non grata around Hollywood right now, but once the press forgot about her, the studios might remember her screenplay. She needed to do some rewriting, tinkering.

Tommy was still insistent that he wanted to play the lead, and maybe an announcement that the two of them were going to be working together might throw some water on the fiery gossip. Since she hadn't ever conceived of him in the role, she wanted to go back over the script and tweak it, make it more suitable for him.

The more she'd thought about it, the more she'd realized he really would be right for the part. She just needed to change her dark, brooding, angry hero into a golden-haired angel whose good looks hid a dangerous, edgy soul. Plus, at least with Tommy, there shouldn't be any diva actor fits over the homoerotic threesome scene!

"What do you do, anyway?" he asked.

"I'm a writer."

He turned his head to look at her from behind the dark glasses. "Novels?"

"Not yet. I was a journalist when I lived in New York. I worked for one of the big papers and hated it. So earlier this year, I moved out to L.A. to market an original screenplay."

"Wow. Any luck?"

"Yes." *And no.* "There's some interest but nothing concrete yet."

"That's pretty amazing. Have you met any stars? Done the whole elite-Hollywood-decadence thing?"

Chuckling, she admitted, "A few. And maybe a little decadence." Then, remembering what he'd said yesterday about having two all-inclusive packages, she asked the question that had been flitting around in her mind.

"So, what about you? Why the solo vacation—and the two-person package?"

He sighed audibly, turning his head to look at the pool again. She lifted her drink, sucking some of the delicious sweetness through the straw, giving him time. She wondered for a moment if he was going to ignore the question, but finally, he cleared his throat.

"This was supposed to be my honeymoon."

She coughed out a mouthful of her drink, spewing it onto her own bare shoulder. Sitting up straighter in the chair, she coughed a few more times.

"Are you okay?" he asked.

He'd sat right up and swung around to face her, patting her back as if helping a kid spit out too big a mouthful of food. Well, she had to concede, that had been a lot to digest. Even in the crazy moment, when her mind had begun to spin over the whole idea that Leo was supposed to be here with another woman—his *wife*—she had time to think how nice his strong fingers had felt on her back.

"I'm fine," she insisted, nodding and scrunching her eyes closed. Some of her drink had flown out of her mouth, some she'd gulped down, and now she had a damned brain freeze. "I was just surprised."

"Sorry."

Finally, when she felt in full control of herself, she turned to face him. Their bare legs brushed against each other, their feet inches apart on the stone pool deck. The coarse black hairs on his legs tickled her smooth ones, just another vivid example of his maleness compared to her femininity. The soft sensation made her stomach flip and her bathing suit feel a tiny bit tighter against her groin.

She forced those sensations away to focus on their conversation. "You were supposed to be here with your *wife?*"

"I'm not married!" he assured her.

"Good thing. I mean, considering you came on your honeymoon alone. What happened?"

"Same old story. Long engagement, nonrefundable trip paid for, wedding got canceled."

"So, what, she kept the dress and you kept the trip?"

"Something like that. We returned what we could but both of us ate some of the costs."

"That must have been painful."

"Not too terrible, considering we broke up six months before the wedding date."

Six months. So he wasn't exactly on the rebound. That was good to know.

"But you still couldn't get a refund on this?" She gestured around the grounds.

"Nope. I'd prepaid for a whole honeymoon package. Nonrefundable."

Wow, that had been pretty optimistic, considering how frequently people broke up these days.

He must have read her expression. "I know, I know. I can't imagine what I was thinking. I wasn't just being a cheapskate, I swear. I think, deep down, doing it that way was an affirmation that I believed we really would get married, even though, somewhere deep inside, I'd already begun to have doubts."

"So it was a friendly, mutual breakup?"

He barked a laugh. "Oh, hell, no."

She didn't reply, not asking the natural questions. She'd already been incredibly nosy. If he wanted to share more, he would.

"She cheated."

Oh, no. Stupid, foolish woman.

"I'm so sorry."

Those broad shoulders lifted in a careless shrug. "I'm over it. What hurt the most was that she did it with my best man…can you possibly get more cliché?"

"Or more trashy?" she snapped. "What a bitch."

"It takes two…he's a bitch, too."

His tone held no heat; he didn't seem to be bearing any grudges or holding on to any residual anger. So maybe he really was over all that. He'd certainly seemed to be so far. She would never have guessed he'd been recently betrayed and hurt by someone he'd cared enough about to propose to.

It truly boggled her mind. She had no use for cheaters, anyway, something she'd never been more thoroughly reminded of than when she'd become the country's most infamous one. But to cheat on someone like Leo? She didn't get it. He was impossibly handsome. He was thoughtful, funny and heroic. He was built like a god, kissed like a dream and had hands that should be patented. She couldn't even begin to imagine how amazing he would be in bed…. He certainly had plenty to offer a woman there.

So why on earth would anyone risk that for a fling with someone else? Even more—how could anyone who proclaimed to care about him do something so hateful, so hurtful, to a man who was so wonderful?

"She's insane."

He waved a hand. "It worked out for the best. Maybe she sensed I wasn't as emotionally attached as I should have been. I think part of her wanted me to find out, wanted to see how I'd react and make sure she really was the center of my world. If I'd played the part of enraged, jealous fiancé, she might have felt more certain that I really loved her."

"Oh, genius plan," she said with a big eye roll. As if he'd have ever taken her back after she'd played such a game? What man would? "You didn't, I presume?"

He shook his head slowly. "I was embarrassed, and I punched the guy. I think I was more mad at him!"

"Bros before hos?"

He grinned, not appearing to mind that she'd just called his ex a ho. Then again, the ex was a ho.

"I didn't yell at her, didn't fight, just…left. I told her what I wanted out of the apartment and that I never wanted to see her again. The end."

"Wow," she murmured, suddenly imagining how that must have felt. Whatever punishment his ex had gotten, including the embarrassment and the ending of her engagement, must surely have paled next to the realization that Leo didn't give a damn that she'd cheated on him. Madison honestly didn't know if she could have survived that.

Not, of course, that she would ever cheat on someone to whom she'd committed herself. Except, of course, according to every damned tabloid in the United States.

"Well, all I can say is, she's an idiot."

He chuckled. "Thanks."

"And you're better off."

"Oh, no doubt about that. But I can't help wishing I'd figured it out sooner. Ah, well, lesson learned. If nothing else, it reaffirmed how incredibly lucky I am to be surrounded by people who really *do* love each other."

"Who?"

"My family." His laughter deepened. "My big, huge, obnoxious, pushy, bossy, demanding family."

"You have a lot of siblings?"

"Two brothers, one older, one younger. But also a ton of cousins, aunts, uncles, second cousins, grandparents. My family might inspire a sequel to *My Big Fat Greek Wedding,* only with Italians."

Good grief, there were more Leos in the world? It boggled the mind.

"And they're all happily married?"

"There's been one divorce in the Santori clan in the past ten years, and that was a great-aunt and uncle who got tired of waiting for each other to die."

She snorted.

"Otherwise, everybody's faithful, everybody's happy. They're pretty damned amazing and incredibly lucky." He shrugged. "It's set a standard for me. I almost took a step that wasn't living up to that standard, and I got slapped down for it. I won't make that mistake again."

No, she didn't imagine he would. He would never sell himself short again, that was for sure. Even she knew he'd never commit to a woman he wasn't completely sure about.

Her heart almost wept over that. To be the woman a man this steady, this sure, this *wonderful* really loved would be such a gift. What a miracle.

And, for her, what an impossibility.

Because all Madison could bring to Leo was embarrassment and scandal, and it sounded like he'd had enough of those to last his whole life. She might as well be walking around with a big scarlet *A* sewn to the front of her bathing suit. His association with her could only drag him through the mud.

He didn't deserve that. And she didn't deserve him.

She knew that. But that didn't change one damn thing.

She still wanted him desperately. They didn't have much time, only six more days, but the more time she spent here, the more confident she was of the privacy and security of this place. Maybe it was risky, maybe she was being selfish, but she couldn't deny that the thought of spending six solid days on the grounds of this resort, having a wild, passionate affair with the man sitting next to her, excited her beyond reason.

Should she, though? She'd made so many bad calls lately, had misjudged one situation after another, the most recent being just how interested the world might be in her love life. Could she really entice Leo Santori into a wild, passionate, short-term affair that they could both walk away from, unscathed, next week?

She honestly didn't know. Nor did she know whether she should.

She just knew she *wanted* to.

HAVING BEEN TOLD by the staff to come to the lobby at around six, dressed comfortably, Leo knocked on her door at five minutes before the hour.

"Right on time," she said as she answered.

"Promptness is my specialty."

"I thought snake wrangling was your specialty."

"That's another one," he said with a laugh as she came outside, pulling the door to her bungalow shut behind her.

She stepped out onto the path, into the sunlight, and he took a sharp breath, looking her over, from head to toe.

Madison was wearing a silky, wispy sundress, all color and light. It was strapless, clinging to her full breasts, tight down to her hips, then flaring out, falling to her knees. The bright, tropical colors made her newly tanned skin glow. Her brilliant green eyes were made even more dramatic with heavier makeup than she usually wore, and she'd swept her hair up onto her head in a loose bun, leaving several long curling strands to fall over her bare shoulders.

She wore simple sandals with a small, delicate ankle bracelet. Something about it, that tiny strip of gold, made his heart race. He wanted to take it off, wanted to kiss her ankle and lick her instep and taste his way all the way up the inside of those beautiful thighs.

"Do you think I look okay?" she asked, noticing his silence.

"No. Not just okay. I think you're beautiful," he said.

She smiled, pleased at the compliment, then looked him over. "I think you are too."

He hadn't been lying about the limits of his wardrobe, but he had remembered to pack a pair of khakis and one dress shirt. It wasn't exactly Chicago dress casual, considering he had brown leather thongs on his feet, but he figured it would do for whatever the hotel staff had cooked up.

They needed to go—it was at least a five-minute walk to the lobby. But something made him stop. This wasn't a date; they were simply getting comped a meal for what had happened this morning. But he couldn't go another minute without doing what he'd wanted to do ever since she'd left his arms earlier today.

Without saying a word, he slid his hands into her hair, knowing he was probably going to knock down more of those sexy curls and not caring. He pulled her to him, saw her eyes flare the tiniest bit in surprise, then he covered her mouth with his.

She didn't hesitate but slid her arms up to encircle his neck, holding him close. Madison tilted her head, parting her lips, gently sliding her tongue out to welcome his. They tasted and explored, slowly, lazily, and he realized he hadn't imagined how good things had been with them this morning. They had chemistry; it was instant, undeniable, almost heady. The more they kissed, the more they wanted to. She pressed her body against his, the pebbled tips of her breasts and the musky, female scent rising off her telling him she was every bit as ready to turn back around and go into her room, skipping dinner in favor of the most delicious physical dessert.

But he wasn't in a rush. No rush at all.

Leo liked taking things slow. There would be no mad, crazy, gotta-get-in-you-right-now coupling. Not with this woman. Oh, maybe that would happen someday, but for their first time, he intended to savor every inch of her. For hours.

Finally, knowing they were probably already late, he ended the kiss and drew away from her. He patted her hair back into place, fixed one dangling curl, and said, "I guess we should go."

"You still want to?"

He saw the question in her eyes, knew she was ready to say to hell with dinner, let's order room service. But like a kid who looked forward to the raw anticipation of Christmas Eve far more than the present-orgy of the next morning, he held firm.

"Yeah, I do. Let's go see what they've got cooked up for us."

She frowned a little. To make sure she understood this wasn't in any way a rejection, he brushed his lips across her mouth one more time. "I can't wait to take that dress off you."

Her eyes flew open and she gasped. "Do you think you can just…"

"Yeah, I can. You want me, Madison. It's dripping off you."

She opened her mouth, then snapped it shut. How could she possibly deny something so utterly obvious to them both?

"And that's good," he added. "Because I want you, too. All I can think about when I see the way your nipples are pressing against those red flowers on the fabric is that they'll taste like ripe berries against my tongue."

He couldn't resist reaching up and flicking his fingers against those taut tips, feeling her sway in reaction as he plucked and teased. He wanted to cup and stroke and suck her but there was no time. Not nearly enough time.

"Leo!"

"Yeah. You're going to taste better than anything they put in front of us for dinner."

She gulped, closed her eyes, obviously trying to steady her breaths. He noticed the way she clenched a lightweight shawl in her hands and wondered if she was picturing his neck in her grip. She appeared ready to strangle him for teasing her now, when there was no way he could follow through.

Hell, the woman obviously didn't appreciate the fine art of anticipation.

"I'll make it up to you," he told her. "I'll make it so worth the wait, Madison."

She opened her eyes, looking up at him, her frown softening, her lips curving into a trusting smile. Then, just to show he wasn't the only one who could play the game, she whispered, "If you think my nipples will taste sweet, just wait until you taste the rest of me."

It was his turn to pause for a deep breath.

"I haven't been with anyone in six months, Leo, and I'm dying to be explored, tasted, *taken*."

"Six months? Funny, same with me. Maybe six months is our lucky number."

It was as if they'd both taken a time-out from everyone else just so they could build toward this night, this joining.

"Mmm-hmm. And if I don't have you in me in the next few hours, I think I'll just die."

"A few hours, huh?" He glanced at his watch. "That doesn't leave much time for foreplay."

She hissed and grabbed at his arm, as if her legs had weakened.

"But I suppose I can make do."

She swallowed visibly. "Please, let's just skip dinner."

"Not a chance, beautiful."

Smiling, Leo took her arm and physically turned her toward the pathway, leading her to the lobby. She didn't say anything, and her steps were the tiniest bit wobbly, as if she was still affected by the sultry promise in his words.

Because he *had* been making a promise.

Hours of foreplay? Not a problem. As long as he could lose himself inside of her at the end of it.

The realization that they'd both turned the corner and admitted that this night would end up with them in bed was enough to slake his appetite for now. It would build, hour by hour, until they were back here. And by then, he looked forward to adoring every inch of her body the way it was meant to have been adored every day for the past six cold, lonely months.

7

As it turned out, the staff's "surprise" dinner wasn't in the upscale restaurant attached to the hotel. Nor was there a limo waiting to whisk them off to some fancy place up in Santa Cruz. Nor was there a bevy of staff carrying trays of room service for a poolside rendezvous.

Instead, they were told when they arrived at the lobby a few minutes after six that they would be going on a beach picnic.

They were instructed to head down to a small, secluded beach tucked into a private cove below the hotel, reserved only for guests. Leo had read about it in the brochures, and he and Madison had talked about heading down there tomorrow. Today they'd just soaked up some sun by the pool, talking, laughing, drinking. She'd filled him in a little on the Hollywood scene—ugh. He'd told her about life in the Windy City. More interesting were all the things they'd both been thinking about but hadn't discussed. Things like how she tasted, how her body molded so perfectly against his, fitting him like she'd been made to be his other half.

As they followed the directions, walking down the steps carved into the hillside below the resort, he realized the term *beach picnic* was far too simple and mundane for the reality. This was more like a picnic a sheikh might indulge in somewhere along the Mediterranean.

"Wow, this is stunning," she said as they reached the bottom of the planked steps.

"No kidding."

The water was a little rough, white-capped waves lapping ashore, not as gentle and soft as a typical Caribbean resort. He liked this better; the Pacific seemed wild and powerful, as timeless as the earth. There was nothing placid about it. It was full of passion and energy.

The shoreline was a broad swath of pale sand, not sugar fine, but still clean and beautiful where it met the blue-green edge of the water.

Not only did they have the cove entirely to themselves—it was near sunset, and, he supposed, the few other guests were eating in the restaurant or were already out on the town. But they also would be dining in splendor. He could only wonder at all the trouble the staff had gone to, and couldn't decide whether it was more a result of the snake or the matchmaking front desk clerk.

A flowing canopy, white and lacy, stood in a sheltered area of the beach, nestled near the curving hillside. Fabric twined around each of the four legs, and it billowed in the evening breeze. Beneath it were a small café table and two chairs.

A chef stood at a tabletop grill, beside which were platters stacked with skewered meat, marinating fish and fresh vegetables. The man smiled as they reached the canopy tent and immediately began to grill the food as the uniformed waiter led them to their seats.

A pristine white cloth covered the table. The center was taken up with a beautiful vase full of colorful, tropical blooms, and a bottle of champagne was laid on ice, two glasses at the ready.

"Good lord, this is like the deluxe wedding night meal in the brochure," Madison whispered as the waiter pulled out her chair and she sat down.

He took his own seat and nodded. This was feeling more and more like a setup, and he decided he needed to leave a large tip for the desk clerk when he checked out.

When he saw the bed-size double lounger, draped with soft, white fabric, he decided to make it an extra-large one.

"Glad we came?" he asked.

She cast a quick look at the lounger. "I think I'm going to be."

"I have no doubt you're going to be."

She shivered a little, though the evening was still warm, and a lovely pink color appeared on her tanned throat, as if her body was growing flushed. He looked forward to exploring that soft swath of pink skin later.

Before she could say anything else, they were startled by the strumming of a guitar. They hadn't even noticed the musician sitting a few yards away. He smiled and nodded as he began to play softly, the notes riding on the air, mingling with the call of seabirds and the never-ending churning of the ocean.

"Champagne?" the waiter asked.

They nodded, and he popped the bottle of an expensive vintage, then poured them each a glass.

"I suppose we should offer a toast to something," Madison said once the waiter had discreetly returned to the chef's table, leaving them in privacy.

"I don't imagine we should drink to the sn..."

She threw a hand up, palm out. "Don't say that word! No more mentioning him tonight."

"All right. How about we drink to...new friendships?"

"As in, vacation buddies?"

He shook his head. "That's not the term I'd use."

Their stares met, and the table suddenly seemed even smaller, more intimate. Because Madison's green eyes were glowing with something that went far beyond friendship. This was so much more than that. Whatever was happening between them, however long it might last and wherever it might go, it was about a lot more than either of them were probably ready to admit. Every minute they'd spent together had suggested that. The kiss they'd shared outside her room had reinforced it. Their conversation had cemented it.

"Let's drink to new beginnings," he finally said.

That felt right, at least for him. For the past six months, he'd been living in limbo. It was almost as if a part of him had been waiting for the original wedding date to pass so the reality that it would never happen would finalize itself in his mind. Now that it had happened, now that the day had come and gone, he felt no sadness, no wistfulness. There was only freedom. Relief. And, now that he'd met Madison, pure anticipation.

"I like that," she said, as if she, too, had something she wanted to move beyond.

Although they'd talked for hours today, while they'd enjoyed the pool—swimming, sunbathing, eating a light lunch—she hadn't opened up much about her past. But he sensed she had come here to escape from her troubles, much as he had. As well as seeking something new and different.

Well, they'd found it. Because they'd found each other.

Maybe just for the next few days. It was too soon to tell. But starting tonight, he and Madison Reid were going to become lovers. Of that he had absolutely no doubt.

It had nothing to do with the conversation they'd had before leaving her room, or with the romantic setup... although the bed definitely didn't hurt. Rather, it had everything to do with the tension and awareness that had been building between them from the moment they'd met. Hell, even if he'd been fully dressed when she'd walked into his room yesterday, and she hadn't fainted in his arms and there had been no naked embrace this morning, this thing between them would still be happening.

It was overwhelming his senses, answering all the questions he'd been asking himself for the past several months. And it was making him more certain than he'd been about anything that he'd finally met the kind of woman he'd been waiting for. One who he couldn't stop thinking about, who filled his thoughts and fueled his every desire, until his hand nearly shook with the need to reach out and touch her. Take her.

"Leo?" she asked, her voice soft.

He shook his head, realizing she was watching him expectantly, her glass in her raised hand. He lifted his, too.

"New beginnings," she said.

He echoed her words. They clinked glasses, and both drank.

The champagne went down smoothly, and the conversation was just as smooth. They had fallen into an easy rhythm with one another sometime after they'd met, and as they waited for their meal to be prepared, answering the chef's questions about their preferences, they talked about a lot of nothing. But good nothing. Fine nothing.

Over fresh fruit, they compared family stories. He marveled that she was an identical twin—that there was another woman as beautiful and perfect as this one somewhere in the world.

She teased him about being the middle of three boys, correctly assessing that he'd been the easygoing one who was always smiling. Unlike his older brother, who was an Army Ranger, or his younger one who was a cop, Leo had always been the comedian of the family, the peacemaker.

When they moved on to a salad filled with exotic greens, they'd talked politics. Only a bit—enough to confirm they were both the same shade of light purple, i.e. a little of this, a little of that. Neither of them were militant on any point, though it seemed important to her that he agree with her on civil rights and gay marriage, which he did.

They didn't talk much when the grilled mahi, marinated beef skewers and crisp vegetables arrived, too focused on the perfection of the meal. And afterward, when the waiter delivered enormous strawberries freshly dipped in chocolate, he couldn't find anything to say. He was too busy watching the way those full lips of hers looked drenched in chocolate, wondering if she cooed like that and closed her eyes with pure, visceral pleasure when she had sex.

He was going to find out tonight.

Their eyes kept meeting. Their hands touched when they both reached for the butter or the water. Their legs brushed. And minute after minute, the pleasurable tension rose. He felt it. She felt it, too. She broadcast it with every flick of her tongue across her lips, every intentional tilt of her head, sweep of her lashes and the tiny sighs she couldn't contain when he leaned close to taste something off her plate or when she reached over to brush a crumb off his shirt.

Tension. Oh, such delightful tension.

"Would you like coffee?" the waiter asked after he'd cleared away the last of the dishes. The chef had already departed, after they'd extended their sincere thanks, and the musician was packing up his guitar.

"That would be nice, thanks," Madison said. She pulled her wrap around her shoulders. The sun had begun to set, the evening air gaining more of a chill.

After serving the coffee, the waiter walked out from under the canopy to light some tiki torches that had been planted in the sand. When he returned, he said, "Please enjoy the sunset. Staff will be down to clean up later tonight. It's been a pleasure serving you, and again, the management extends its sincere apologies for today's inconvenience."

"Thank you," Madison replied, and Leo echoed the sentiment.

Then the man departed, the guitarist following him. Leo and Madison were left alone on the tiny beach.

Without a word, he rose from his seat and extended a hand. When she took it, he helped her stand and led her to the plush lounger. Pulling her with him, he sat down on it, spread out, and helped her tuck herself in beside him. She was on her side, her head on his shoulder, one thigh lifted and curled between his, her hand traipsing lazy circles on his chest.

The sun slipped farther, ever farther, and they remained quiet, washed in the glory of it. There was no need for conversation. They both simply knew, somehow, that the moment deserved utter silence, the only sounds those of their beating hearts and the churning waves.

Red and orange beams chased each other over the surf as the massive golden orb descended toward the horizon. They began to dance across the water, sent forth from some far-off, mystical place, thousands of lines of light riding the waves and landing close to their feet. The entire world seemed to be made of glistening light, every droplet of water in the spray turned into a jeweled rainbow.

Against his chest, he felt Madison stop breathing, and understood the reason. He found himself holding his breath, too, as that globe dropped what seemed like inches into the vast blue. Farther. Farther. Until at last, with a final wink and a flash, it fell off the edge of the world.

She exhaled in a rush. "Beautiful."

It had been. "A once in a lifetime sundown."

Which seemed appropriate for the once in a lifetime night they were about to begin.

AFTER THE SUN had descended beyond the horizon, Madison remained curled up against Leo, content to relive the beauty of the moment in her mind. She'd never seen a more glorious sunset.

Leo remained quiet, too, content to watch, and to stroke lazy circles on her back with his fingers. Her shawl had slipped down and there was nothing separating his fingertips from her sensitive skin, which grew more sensitive with each gentle stroke.

But despite being gentle, there was nothing simple or innocent about it. The same rapt attention she'd paid to the sunset now shifted and turned, zoning in on the feelings he was arousing in her with that deliberate touch. Every time his hand moved a tiny bit lower, pushing closer to the back of her sundress, she shimmied up a little, wanting those fingers to push the material away, to bare her to the cool evening air and the heat of his touch.

Though the sun was gone, darkness certainly hadn't descended. The sky was still awash with purple, orange and gold. Once it did grow dark, the torches would still provide enough illumination for them, though not for anyone standing high on the cliffs above them to actually look down and see them. Especially not beneath the graceful canopy.

The scene was designed for private seduction. For intimacy. And while she couldn't totally agree that the woman at the front desk was doing some matchmaking, she couldn't rule it out, either. Because this setting was simply too perfect for sensual interludes to be accidental.

"You warm enough?" he asked.

"I'm perfect."

He shifted, rolling onto his side to face her, looking intently into her eyes. "Yes, you are."

Placing the tip of his index finger on her chin he tilted her head up, then bent down to brush his lips against hers.

Madison had been in a state of high alert all evening. Hell, all day—ever since that wild, erotic encounter on the patio. She had been thinking of nothing else but being possessed by him—taken wildly, roughly, desperately.

But now, she realized, she wanted it slow. Wanted a lingering, deep kiss that lasted at least a hundred heartbeats, and wanted it to end only because there was so very much more to explore.

He seemed to read her mind. He kept the kiss slow, lazy and sensual, his warm tongue exploring her mouth thoroughly. He tasted every bit of her, breathing into her and taking her breath.

A hundred heartbeats passed. At least. Or perhaps a thousand. Time began to lose its meaning as darkness fell and the night became lit by only those torches and the glow of moonlight they could glimpse through the fabric of the canopy.

He finally moved his lips away, kissing the corner of her mouth. He moved to her cheek, tasting her jawline, and then her neck, until he was breathing into her ear, his tongue flicking out to sample the lobe.

"I've wanted you from the minute you fell into my arms and fainted," he whispered.

"I've wanted you since I walked into the room and saw you standing there."

"Finest male ass you've ever seen," he said with a laugh.

"I can't deny it."

She stretched a little, arching against him, sliding her bare leg up and down against him. Leo moved a hand down her arm, blazing a trail of heat against her cool skin, awakening every nerve ending. He was still focused on her neck, and he kissed his way down it, until he could bury his face in her neck. There he paused to inhale, breathing her in, as if intoxicated by her essence.

She twined her fingers in his hair, needing something to hold on to when he resumed his slow study of her body. Without a word, he reached up to the elastic top of her dress and tugged it down, following the material, kissing every inch of skin as it was revealed. She arched toward his mouth, her breasts heavy, aching and desperate. When the top hem finally scraped across her nipples and popped over them, she moaned. Every stroke was intense, every sensation built upon the last.

He leaned up on an elbow, staring down at her as he pulled the bodice all the way down, revealing her breasts. Even in the semidarkness she could see the hunger in his eyes, the way he had to part his lips to take a shaky breath.

"Taste me," she ordered, knowing he was dying to. He'd been dying to since they'd left her room.

He reached for one breast, cupping it in his hand, plumping it and lightly squeezing her nipple. Heat sluiced through her, as if there were a wire between her breast and her groin, and she jerked reflexively.

Leo didn't notice, he was far too focused on looking at her, studying her, as if he'd never seen anything more beautiful. The tension stretched and built, and she thought she'd die if he didn't suckle her. When she'd almost reached the point of begging, he bent to flick his tongue over her sensitive nipple.

"Oh, God, yes," she cried, waves of heat washing ever downward.

He needed no more urging, moving to cover her entire nipple with his mouth. His hot breath seared her, then he was closing tight, his lips capturing her, his tongue flicking out to taste. He sucked hard, making all her nerve endings roar.

She reached for his shirt, desperate to feel him, and ripped at the front. A few buttons flew, enough for her to reach in and stroke his powerful chest, feel the sheen of sweat on his body that spoke of hunger and desire and need far more than the temperature of the air.

He continued to suckle her, reaching for her other breast, stroking and squeezing it, playing with her nipple until she shook.

"Berries," he murmured. "Sweet and so pretty."

As if remembering she'd invited him to taste far more than her nipples, he finally moved down and kissed a slow path over her midriff. He sampled each rib, licking each indentation, scraping his teeth across her skin as he pulled the dress out of his way.

When it got down to her hips, she lifted up a little so he could pull it all the way off. Beneath it, she wore only a tiny, skimpy pair of panties, lacy and white, the kind made to be torn off by a hungry man. They might as well have been advertised that way on the package.

"Pretty," he said as he studied them. Closely. His mouth was beneath her belly button, his jaw rubbing against the elastic of her panties. She felt his warm breaths through the nylon, and arched up in welcome.

He moved farther, placing his open mouth on her mound and inhaling deeply, breathing her in through the material.

"Oh, God, Leo," she cried, dying—just dying—for him to lick every inch of her.

As if knowing she'd taken about as much as she could, he began to uncover her fully. But he didn't tear the panties off, he merely tugged them, slowly, inch by inch, watching closely as he revealed her secrets.

"Oh, man," he whispered, his voice shaking as he looked at her.

She smiled. He liked what he saw.

He proved it, pushing the panties the rest of the way off, and then reaching for one of her legs. He stroked her thigh gently before pushing it, parting her legs, opening them so he could enjoy her in all her wantonness.

There was no thought of shyness, no modesty, nothing but heat and desire, natural and earthy. He looked at her as if he'd never seen anything more beautiful and moved immediately to taste her.

His mouth moved to her sex, his lips gliding against her in an erotic kiss that defied description. He licked her thoroughly, scraping his warm, wet tongue all over her outer lips, then slipping into the folds for more.

A helpless, desperate cry escaped her mouth. It was carried off by the night breeze, and she wondered just how many more times the man would make her cry out tonight.

"Beautiful," he said, touching her, stroking her, gently plucking at each secret place so he could study her more intimately.

He flicked the tip of his index finger over her clit, which throbbed with sensation, then moved his mouth to it and sucked it gently. As if he knew her body already, he circled his finger around the base while he flicked her with his tongue. Everything—all sensation, all desire, all need—centered there. It built and throbbed until it finally exploded in a climax that left her shaking so hard her teeth chattered.

He noticed. Kissing his way back up her body, until he reached her face, he murmured, "Are you cold?"

"Oh, God, no," she replied, wrapping her arms around him.

He kissed her deeply, his mouth tasting like sex and desire, and she reached again for his shirt, determined not to be stopped by a few buttons this time.

Leo broke away long enough to take over the task, yanking the thing up and over his head and tossing it to the sand. She bit her lip, watching as he quickly undid his khakis, waiting to see that amazing erection she'd held in her hand just this morning.

He rose onto his knees, pushing his pants down. He hadn't been wearing anything underneath, and all her breath left her body in a deep, hungry groan.

"I didn't imagine it," she managed to whisper.

He didn't say anything, but focused on pushing his pants all the way off. Then he returned his full attention to her.

Madison parted her legs even farther in an age-old invitation to claim her. Fill her.

"I'm on the pill," she told him when he paused, opening his mouth as if about to ask her something. "And there's nothing else for you to worry about."

"Or for you," he said.

Then there was no more talking. Nothing else to say. The only communicating they needed to do was with their bodies.

He moved between her parted thighs, bracing himself above her and staring down at her face. Just to melt her heart a tiny bit more, to reinforce the goodness she'd sensed in the man from the beginning, he asked, "You're sure? No second thoughts, no regrets?"

She reached up and encircled his shoulders, drawing him down to her. "I've never been more sure about anything."

"Neither have I," he admitted as he settled between her legs, nudging her sex with that massive erection that both thrilled and intimidated her.

She shouldn't have worried. He was careful, gentle, and he'd aroused her to the point of insanity. She was dripping wet, soft, welcoming and so ready to be filled by him.

He knew. And he began to fill her.

He slid into her warm opening, the passage easy and smooth. All the feminine parts of her reacted and responded the way they were supposed to, with utter surrender to pleasure. She clenched him, tugging him deeper, both with her arms and with her sex. Leo groaned, letting himself be taken in, still careful, but obviously starting to lose himself to sensation.

"Yes. Take me," she pleaded, tightening her arms around his neck, nipping at his throat. "Take me *now.*"

That drove him onward. Without another word, he arched his hips and plunged, driving into her more deeply than she'd ever thought it possible to go. She let out another cry of pure, utter satisfaction, and focused on savoring the sensation of heat and power and such wonderful, delightful fullness.

"Are you…"

"I'm fine," she said, moving her mouth to his and licking his lips for entry.

They kissed hungrily, tongues entwining, and he slowly pulled out of her, only to sink again. She arched up to meet the slow thrust, curving her hips upward, wrapping her legs around those lean flanks.

"Madison," he whispered, still cautious.

"More," she demanded, knowing why he was being so careful, knowing he was afraid to hurt her. "Don't take it easy on me, Leo, I *want* it. Give it to me."

She tightened her hands in his hair, gripping him, almost at the point of begging him to pound and thrust.

And then he began to pound and thrust.

He pulled out and drove back in, going deeper and deeper. The walls of her sex wrapped around him, taking everything, greedy for more. Her heart pounded wildly and she found it hard to catch her breath. She couldn't think, couldn't focus, could only *be*.

Leo had obviously thrown off the last of his restraints, because he suddenly rolled over onto his back, pulling her with him. He sat her up, impaling her on his cock, holding tightly to her hips.

"Yeah, baby, please," she groaned, digging her fingers into the crisp hair on his chest.

He encircled her waist with his hands and thrust up, just as he tugged her down. The intensity was wild, and he bored a path even deeper into her. She let out a little scream, but when he paused, she glared down at him. "Don't you stop. Don't you dare stop."

"Not planning on it, sweetheart," he said between harsh breaths.

The muscles in his chest and arms clenched and flexed and his jaw was like granite. His eyes closed and he dropped his head back as he thrust up into her again. And again. And again.

Although she was on top, he controlled their every move, handling her as easily as if she'd been a doll. But she didn't care. Every movement he made was for her pleasure. As if to reinforce that, he moved one hand between them and rubbed her clit, just to make sure she'd climax again when he was ready to.

The heat began to rise again, the sensations spiraled. She was battered by the cool evening air, completely filled with his rock-hard cock, gripped and held and completely lost to pure sexual bliss.

And when he finally gave a hoarse shout, indicating he'd gained his own, she followed him to an explosive orgasm, and then collapsed onto his body, boneless, weak and exhausted.

8

As it turned out, Leo hadn't merely paid for an "all-inclusive" meal plan he didn't need, he'd apparently paid for an unneeded room, too. After he and Madison had become lovers on the beach, they had, by unspoken agreement, gone back to her room and slept together in her bed.

The sex was phenomenal.

Sleeping together afterward just made it better.

He liked drifting off with her head resting against his shoulder, her arm curled over his middle, their legs entwined. He liked it even better every time he woke up to find her warm beside him, ready for more.

They'd spent the deepest, darkest hours of the night exploring each other in a slow, sultry orgy of lust that seemed to go on forever. Or, at least, as long as he could hold out. Madison had once again proved to be impatient, as greedy in bed as she was generous out of it. At one point, he'd been able to do nothing but laugh—and comply—when she'd demanded that he stop with all the oral sex and just fuck her into the headboard.

Hoping to start the day off the same way, he reached for her as soon as he woke up the next morning. Her half of the bed was empty. It was warm, though, as if she'd just left it a few moments ago. Sitting up, he glanced toward the bathroom. The door was open, but she wasn't inside.

A muffled voice was talking nearby, and he finally glanced out the patio door and saw her sitting in the sunshine, talking on her phone.

She was stark naked.

Damn, he liked this place.

Beams of sunlight illuminated every delicious bit of her, catching all the gold highlights in that honey-brown hair. He'd touched and kissed almost every inch of her last night, but he hadn't seen her in all her glory until this moment, and the sight of her nearly stopped his heart. She was all softness and curves and smooth, silky skin.

And he'd left his mark on her.

Even from here he could see the slightly reddened spots on her throat and breasts, left there by his hungry mouth. There was a small bruise on one hip, and he suspected he'd held her a little too tightly when she'd been riding him.

He didn't feel too badly, though, suspecting that if he looked at his back in the mirror he'd see plenty of war wounds, too. He certainly felt them. But he didn't regret one damn thing. The memory that he could get her out of her mind, raking at him, begging him, and utterly helpless to do anything but take what he gave her turned him on almost as much as looking at her sitting naked in the sunshine.

Smiling, he got up and stretched, not surprised to see he had some major morning wood. Hell, just thinking of her was enough to make him want to go outside and push her legs apart. He couldn't think of a better way to scrape up his knees than kneeling in front of her. Draping her legs over the arms of her chair would put all those beautiful, slick secrets right in front of his face; he wanted to see, explore and taste her all over again.

But she seemed pretty involved in her conversation. So he instead headed to the bathroom to wash up. When he came out, she was still outside, still talking, and he went over and pulled the patio door open.

"No, I swear, I'm fine," she was saying into her cell phone. "You don't need to do anything right now, just let it go. It'll die down, these things always do."

Not sure whether her conversation was a private one or not, he was about to close the door again when she glanced up, saw him standing there and offered him a bright good-morning smile.

"Hi," he murmured, bending down to kiss the top of her head.

"Hi back," she replied before returning to her telephone conversation. "What? Uh, yeah. Someone I met here in Costa Rica."

Ah, she was explaining him to someone.

"Oh, be quiet, you know-it-all," she said good-naturedly. "Of course he's hot."

He snickered.

"Leo. Like the lion."

Rowr.

She sighed heavily, obviously getting the third degree. "No, not DiCaprio for God's sake!"

He laughed.

"Yeah, yeah, you're a genius. It was great advice. Blah, blah, blah."

So this someone had been after her to have a wild, sexy fling during her vacation? Interesting, considering that was also what his friends had told him to do, which made him wonder again what it was that haunted Madison. They hadn't discussed it, beyond her admission that she'd come here to get away from her troubles for a while. What were those troubles, though? Had her friends told her to go off and have an affair to get over a broken heart? And if so, who'd broken it?

The idea of someone hurting her made his whole body stiffen in anger. He walked over to the pool's edge, not wanting her to interpret his reaction as jealousy.

Even if, he had to concede, that might be part of it.

Yeah, he hated the idea that anyone might have hurt her.

But it was more than that. The very thought of any other man having his hands on her, making her cry out in pleasure the way she had for him last night, made him want to punch the bungalow wall. How crazy was that? He was jealous over somebody she might have been with even before she'd met him? He'd only known her a couple of days, but the very idea of it made him more ready to do violence than the reality of his former best man sleeping with his ex-fiancée.

"You are losing it, man," he muttered.

"Did you say something?"

He hadn't even realized she'd ended her call and walked up behind him until she spoke. Before he could turn around, she'd slipped her arms around his waist and stepped in close, hugging him from behind. Every bare inch of her body delighted him, but, to be honest, he'd rather be the one coming at her from behind.

Hmm. Nice mental images filled his head.

"I just checked," he told her. "The pool is reptile-free and ready to go."

She shivered against his back, her pert nipples scraping his skin, driving him a little nuts. "Yikes, thanks for reminding me. I'd managed to forget all about that this morning."

He turned around, lining the hug up better. Full frontal under the full sun…it was kind of spectacular.

"Sorry I slept so late. You didn't have to go outside to take your call," he said.

"No problem. It was just a friend from California." She smiled broadly, her eyes twinkling with humor in the sunlight. "Before I came here, he had suggested I find a beach bum to hook up with on my vacation. He was very happy to hear your voice and realize I'd taken his advice."

Thrusting off the quick flash of jealousy that her friend was male, Leo pretended to be offended. "Beach bum?"

"Well, no, I guess I have *slightly* higher standards."

"I'm going to have to punish you for that."

"Promises, promises." Her saucy tone and pursed lips said she was thinking of naughty punishments.

Which sounded just fine to him. God, how he enjoyed this woman's blunt approach to everything, from life to sex. He'd never been with anyone who was so open about what she wanted and what she didn't. And when she did or didn't want them.

"Are you, by any chance, a little wicked?"

"Haven't you figured that out by now?"

He stared into her eyes. "I'm getting the picture."

"Are you liking what you see?"

"Yeah." He raked a slow, thorough stare down her body, from the long hair draping her shoulders and playing peekaboo with those pebbled nipples, to the slim middle, to those eminently grippable hips and drool-inspiring long legs. All naked. All completely his, for now at least. "Oh, *hell,* yeah."

"Good. As for the punishment, despite some curiosity, I'm fairly certain I'm not into pain," she explained. "If you ever spanked me, I would probably cut your hand off."

Chuckling, he replied, "No interest in spanking, sweetheart."

She continued. "Nor am I into rape fantasies. Any man who tries to force me won't lose a hand, he'll lose what he uses that hand to play with."

He didn't play along by grimacing, cringing or feigning horror at the idea of losing every man's most prized possession. Instead, he grew serious, reaching out to touch her hair. It was warm beneath his fingertips, baked in the sun. "Every Santori man was raised by a Santori mother who taught him how to treat women.

Lesson number one—men who hurt women are cowards," he said. "I'd never do anything to hurt you."

She turned her face to kiss his palm. "I know that, Leo. I know you'd never really hurt me." Her impish smile returned. "But if you wanted to, say, get a little creative with some…"

Positions? Toys?

"…handcuffs…I might not object."

He coughed into his fist. Jesus, the woman was killing him here.

"Problem?"

"Nope. No problem. Kind of hard to get handcuffs down here, I imagine." He could hear the heat in his tone as he speculated, "We might have to make do with silk scarves or something."

It was her turn to look affected by the conversation. She was breathing across open lips and her eyelids had dropped to half-mast. She might have been teasing, trying to arouse him with some suggestive ideas, but those ideas were obviously exploding into full-fledged X-rated movies in her mind.

"That could be arranged."

"And maybe then you'd have to shut up and wait and take what I want to give you."

"Maybe," she said, completely unrepentant for being so demanding.

Oh, hell, who was he kidding? He loved that she was so demanding. Loved that he got her so worked up she couldn't do anything but scream and beg and threaten him if he didn't proceed. She'd gone so far as to call him a clit tease last night. He couldn't say he'd ever heard the expression, but had to admit, he'd found it pretty funny. And he'd been determined to live up to it.

"Maybe I'll punish you by making you wait all day for your punishment."

"That'd be punishment for you, too," she said, her voice almost a purr.

He knew she was taunting him, and decided to pay her back. Not warning her, he swung her up into his arms, bracing her under the shoulder, crossing-the-threshold style. As she squealed, he stepped to the very edge of the pool, dangling her over the crystal clear water. "Ready to get wet?"

"Don't you dare!" She twined her arms tightly around his neck. "It's too early, the water's too cold."

"Not for a beach bum."

"Superhot fireman, that's what I meant to say. Strong, professional, determined, hardworking hero." Loosening her grip, she traced the tip of her finger across his lips. "Please don't throw me into that cold water, Leo. Pretty please?"

"What are you going to give me if I don't?"

She thought about it, tapping the tip of her finger on her mouth. Then, smiling as if the proverbial lightbulb had just gone off in her head, she replied, "A blow job?"

He was torn between laughing and groaning with pure want. He'd already been aroused and another ten gallons of blood rushed to his cock just at her suggestion.

"You always say what you're thinking, don't you?"

"Pretty much," she admitted. "That's why my closest

friends always called me Mad. It wasn't just a shortening of my name."

"Hmm. Mad. You don't seem like the angry type."

"Not angry. It's short for Mad, Bad and Dangerous to Know."

"That I can see." He glanced at the glistening water, as if he really had to think about it, and said, "Okay, Mad. I guess I won't toss you in this time."

"You really are my hero."

She leaned up and brushed her lips against his. He immediately opened his mouth and deepened the kiss, invading her, taking the sassiness right off her tongue. Madison needed to be kissed, well and often, if only as a reminder that she wasn't always in charge.

When they finally ended the kiss, they were both panting. But he wouldn't put her down yet. He liked holding her, liked being in control for now. She might demand what she wanted, but he was making it pretty damned clear that, physically, he had her right where he wanted her.

She twined her fingers in his hair and looked up at him, her expression purely happy. "That's a very nice way to start the day."

"I had another one in mind when I woke up."

"Sorry I wasn't there."

"It's okay. Like I said, I slept too late anyway. I never sleep so late in the morning unless I'm on nights and have just gone to bed."

"I figured you could use your rest. You got quite a workout last night."

He scrunched his brow, as if giving it careful consideration. "Really?" Lifting her up and down a couple of times in his arms like a barbell, he added, "Funny, I feel great."

She squealed a little and hung on to his shoulders, saying, "That's good. Because I think you're going to get another one today."

"One?"

"Four."

He barked a laugh, then thought about it. Four. Hmm. Not very impressive. "Come on, challenge me, babe."

"Am I going to need to do any walking for the rest of this vacation?" she asked.

He tilted his head, as if considering it. "Not that I can think of."

"Okay, then. I *guess* you can go for a world record."

"What's the record?"

"Twenty-seven."

He snorted. "Yeah, uh, by that point you wouldn't be able to put your legs together, much less walk. And I wouldn't have a dick, much less one capable of getting hard."

She licked her lips, her expression evil. "Back to that blow job idea, are we?"

He didn't tease her back. She'd mentioned that one too many times for him to pretend he wasn't dying for her to use her beautiful mouth on every inch of him.

"I think we could fit that in today, if you really want to."

"I already know it's not going to fit," she said with a smirk. "But I do really want to and I'm always ready to give it the old college try."

"Rah-rah. So, where does that leave us? Somewhere between four and twenty-seven, with a blow job and a serious licking in between?"

She swallowed visibly. "*Serious* licking?"

"Oh, very serious."

"I noticed you kind of like that."

"No, honey, I kind of love it. You taste better to me than anything I've ever eaten in my life."

"Mmm." She wriggled in his arms, obviously reacting to this verbal foreplay.

So was he. In fact, he couldn't lower her to her feet right now because, if he did, she would hit a major obstacle on her way down.

"Okay, then. We're agreed," she said, as if firming up terms for a business proposition.

"We are? What's the final number again?"

"Six." She quickly added, "Plus the licking and the blowing."

Six. She was challenging him to make love to her six times today. Plus the…extras.

No sweat.

He was twenty-eight. His job kept him in peak physical condition. Until last night, he'd been celibate for six long months.

And he was hotter for her than any man had ever been hot for a woman.

Six would be absolutely no hardship.

"And if it'll *really* kill you not to suck my nipples until I scream, I guess you can do that, too," she said, doing him a very great favor by offering up her beautiful breasts for his devouring.

He lifted her higher, bent his head and flicked his tongue over one pretty tip.

"Thank you, that's so selfless of you," he murmured as she sighed with pleasure.

"That's just how I roll."

They both started to laugh, softly at first, then growing louder. There wasn't another woman he could *ever* remember talking to like this, especially one he'd been holding naked in his arms, whose nipple he'd just licked. She was so damned open and quick, witty and confident. Most women he'd dated hadn't been able to take a joke that *wasn't* about sex, much less any that were.

Before Madison, sex had always been twice as serious but only half as good. Adding warm humor to intimacy—at least before the brain cells evaporated and lust took over completely—enhanced the experience in ways he'd never thought possible. Hell, just having a woman smile up at him tenderly, twining her fingers in his hair, was incredible all on its own. As demanding as she could be in bed, Madison still surprised him with moments like those. Every woman he'd ever been with before had been entirely serious, and, he suspected, focused on gaining advantage in the relationship outside of the bedroom.

He and Madison didn't have a relationship—not yet, anyway, not in the real world. This was a vacation fling, although something inside him rebelled at calling it that. Still, it was a freeing proposition; neither of them were playing games, keeping score or exchanging in any kind of tit for tat.

It was easy with Madison. Hot, incredibly hot, but just so easy.

"Okay, then, I think we have a deal," he finally said.

"This is going to be quite a day, isn't it?" Her eyes were wide, gleaming with excitement, and she was practically panting each breath. He could feel the thudding of her heart in her chest and drew her a little more tightly against his body, knowing now where he intended to put her down.

On the bed.

"I think it would be quite a day even if we had to stop after one," he replied, wondering if she heard the tenderness in his voice and correctly interpreted it.

He wanted to spend the day with her. Yes, that day would include a lot of mind-blowing sex. But even if it didn't, he would still be looking forward to it. Just being with her, getting to know her, hearing that laugh, watching those green-gold eyes sparkle in the sun…sounded like the perfect vacation day to him.

She nodded slowly, silently agreeing with him. "Maybe we could just go on and on for hours and call it one."

"Sounds good to me."

Slowly loosening her arms from around his neck, she said, "Don't you want to put me down?"

"In a minute."

He walked across the patio and went inside through the open door. Carrying her to the huge bed, he didn't so much lower her as toss her onto it. Madison stared up at him, those eyes flashing in challenge, and reached for him.

He shook his head slowly.

"What?"

"Move up," he ordered her, nodding toward the pillows.

She did, edging closer to the headboard. When she was close enough, he said, "Get all the way up on your knees. Turn around facing the wall and hold on to the headboard."

She caught her lip between her teeth. He knew this was driving her crazy, both with lust, and because his tone of voice brooked no disobedience. He was calling the shots for now. It was about time she figured that out.

She didn't move. Neither did he.

He could outwait her, of that he had no doubt. Knowing how to prove he could take care of his needs a little more easily than she could right now, he reached down and grabbed his cock. Encircling it in his hand, he stroked. It wasn't nearly as good as she would be, but it got the job done. She hissed, her gaze dropping so she could stare, and he saw her lick her lips.

She made as if to move toward him. He put a hand up to stop her. "Me first. Then your turn."

That was when she finally figured out what he wanted. A sultry smile broke over her face. She stopped stalling, rose to her knees and crawled toward the head of the bed.

Just because she was a witch and she knew how badly he wanted her, she put some serious wag in that ass, parting her legs a little more than was necessary. A flash of glimmering pink—oh, how that smooth skin felt against his lips, he could have died of sensory overload last night—greeted him. She was practically daring him to resist. She wanted him to climb onto the bed behind her on his knees and ram into her.

"Later," he promised.

"Everything's later," she grumbled.

"So stop stalling so we can get on to the now," he said with a lazy grin.

She grinned back, admitting she liked this push and pull between them, the sparring over who called the shots.

She finally reached the top of the bed, shoving the pillows out of her way and kneeling. He walked closer, took her hands and rested them on the top of the tall wooden headboard, making sure she remained on her knees but completely upright.

Kissing her on the mouth, hot and hard, he dropped onto his back on the bed and slid up toward her. "Show me, Mad. Show me everything."

She looked down at him, over her shoulder, and slowly eased her legs apart, opening for him.

"Beautiful," he growled, unable to tear his eyes off her glistening, sensitive folds. She was swollen and plump, pink and perfect.

When her knees were far enough apart to accommodate him, he slid all the way up so his head was between her thighs.

"Hold on tight," he said.

"Is it going to be a bumpy ride?"

"Uh-huh."

"Oh, good. That's my favorite kind."

He didn't give her any more time to prepare or talk.

He just couldn't wait to taste her fully. Wrapping his arms around her thighs, he tilted her sex toward his mouth and slaked his thirst for her.

She cried out when he flattened his tongue and licked her from stem to stern. Knowing he had her attention, he slid his tongue deeper, between those luscious folds. He lapped into her, sliding his tongue deep enough to make her sing, then moving out again. She tasted as amazing as she looked, as she smelled, as she felt, and he had to tell her so.

"I could do this every day for the rest of my life and die a happy man," he muttered.

"You're killing me, Leo," she groaned, sounding hopeless and desperate.

Almost laughing, he moved his mouth to her pebbled clit and sucked it between his lips. Her hips jerked, but he held her tight, nowhere near ready to let her do what he knew she wanted to do: slide down his body and impale herself on him. Although part of him would love that, considering his need was almost painful, he wasn't going there until she'd completely lost herself to everything but sensation.

Continuing the relentless assault, he brought her higher and higher. She quivered and moaned, but didn't release her death grip on the headboard. He explored her completely, pleasured her until his tongue ached, until, finally, a cry of utter satisfaction signaled her orgasm.

"Yes, oh, lord, yes," she said, her voice weak.

He moved out from under her, his face wet, his every sense filled with her. Madison sagged against the headboard, sucking in deep, needy breaths, completely wrung out. She made as if to turn around, and he knew she still wanted to use her mouth on him, but he was barely holding it together. He had to be inside her, right now.

Rising to his knees, he moved in behind her. Madison smiled at him over her shoulder, suddenly looking a lot more energetic, and scooted back to meet him, her legs parted invitingly.

"Yes," she told him. "I want you to be buried so deep inside me I'll remember you there for a week."

He smirked. "A week? Oh, please."

She licked her lips and curved that gorgeous ass a little higher in welcome. He didn't need any further invite. Taking her hips in his hands, he held her tight and nudged into her. Pleasure washed over him the moment hot, hard cock met warm, slick channel, and he groaned as he sank deeper and deeper, every inch feeling like a step closer to heaven.

She cried out when he finally sank all the way, making a place for himself deep inside her willing body.

"You okay?"

She literally purred. "So okay."

Not wanting to hurt her, and knowing the angle had to be pretty intense for her, he moved slowly at first. He made easy love to her, caressing her hips, her thighs and the small of her back between each deep stroke. But as the intensity built, as her cries increased and she pushed back ever harder, he knew she was long past any need or desire for gentleness.

Which was good. Because he'd reached the point where he needed to pound into her in a mindless frenzy.

But he also wanted to see her beautiful face, wanted to kiss her and share the gasps as they both hit that cliff and flew off it.

Pulling out of her, he flipped her onto her back. Her eyes were sparkling with excitement and wanton pleasure. Her face was flushed, her every breath a gasp, and her whole body sheened with sweat. They were slick and hot and so well matched he wondered how he'd ever done this with anyone else.

"That was…"

"The halfway point," he muttered, making sure she knew they weren't done. "At most."

A sultry smile widened those lips. "One-twelfth of our day, then, huh? You'd better slow down."

He laughed out loud, but grew serious when she reached for him, wrapping her arms tightly around his neck and pulling him down for a deep, hungry kiss. Her thighs parted again and he settled between them, getting back into her with one hot, hard plunge. He reached for one of her slim legs, lifting it over his shoulder, lightly biting the thigh as he drove a little deeper. The angle was incredible. He felt so completely taken in by her, welcomed and pleasured.

She thrust her hips to meet his every downward stroke. Soon she was rolling her head back and forth on the pillow, biting her lip to try to hold back her cries.

"Nobody can hear you, sweetheart," he told her as he felt waves of heat radiating through his body, preparing him for a mind-numbing explosion.

As if she'd just been waiting for permission, she let out a tiny scream of pleasure with the next thrust. An even louder one followed, and he knew by the way her head fell back and her fingers tightened, digging into his shoulders, that she had come again. Seeing her losing herself to glorious pleasure was enough to send him tipping over the edge, too, and with one more deep thrust, he flew apart as well, coming into her in wave after wave of ecstasy.

He didn't roll off her right away, wanting to watch sanity return to her face and feel the raging heartbeat begin to slow to a normal rhythm. He lowered her leg, keeping himself propped on his elbows so he didn't crush her, sharing heaving breaths and then, when she opened her eyes again, satisfied smiles.

"That," he told her, "was…"

"Number one."

9

ALTHOUGH THEY HADN'T hit the world record—whatever that might be, and she doubted it was anywhere near twenty-seven—Madison still found it deliciously difficult to walk the next day. For thirty-six hours, she and Leo hadn't left her room, except to go out into the private pool. They'd ordered room service when hungry, had slept when exhausted, had soaked in the pool when overheated, and had made love so many times, she'd lost count of the positions, sensations and orgasms.

And throughout all of that, she hadn't given more than a passing thought to all the nonsense going on back home. It was like they were living in a completely different world. Things like tabloids and paparazzi and movie stars didn't exist.

Being with Leo had made her troubles disappear.

He was funny and smart, could be bossy, which she liked, and could also be incredibly tender, which she also liked. He was, without a doubt, the most amazing lover she'd ever had. Patient to the extreme, powerful and exciting. But the sex was also playful and fun.

Honestly, she didn't even want to think about what it would be like to give him up at the end of this vacation.

Not that they'd talked about that. Neither of them had mentioned the real world or going back to it. She knew she might be riding a cloud of sexual euphoria, but she was happy to be airborne and didn't want to come back down to earth.

Of course, *this* wasn't exactly what she had in mind.

"I'm sorry, I changed my mind, I don't think I can do it." She heard the nervousness in her own voice and while she hated herself for it, she couldn't prevent it.

"Come on, I know you're not scared of heights. You've been skydiving," Leo said, looking surprised.

"Over North America. Not over the freaking jungle."

It was probably a bad time to get cold feet, considering they had already ridden the party bus several hours to get here. They'd also already paid the exorbitant fee for the double experience—a treetop tour on some swinging wooden walkways, plus zip lining out to a beautiful waterfall in the middle of nowhere. Not to mention they were already standing on a small platform hundreds of feet in the air, getting strapped into harnesses for their zip-line adventure!

She'd been very excited about it, right up until the moment she'd seen a vine dangling from a nearby tree and had a sudden image of a long, slithery animal.

"It's the snake factor," Leo said, understanding immediately.

Yeah. That. Madison had seen that vine, recalled what kinds of creatures made their home in the jungle, and her feet had turned into icicles.

She gulped and nodded. "I want to do this, I really do. It's gorgeous." She spread her arms wide and looked around them at the incredible green canopy blocking out the blue sky above their heads. She truly had never seen such a remarkable palette of different shades of green—her favorite color. Part of her wanted to soar through the sky, to explore the wonders of nature that made this place so different from anywhere back home.

Part of her wanted to carjack the nearest tour bus and hightail it back to the resort.

Because of those pesky snakes.

The guide—young, cute and English speaking—had obviously overheard. "Oh, no, no snakes to worry about, *señorita*."

Madison just lifted a skeptical brow.

The young man shrugged. "Maybe a few."

She reached for the clasp of her harness, ready to strip out of the contraption.

"But you'll do nothing more than wave to them from the air as you fly over," Leo insisted with a chuckle.

"What if the harness breaks and I fall a hundred feet into a nest of fer-de-lances?"

"That won't happen," the guide assured her.

"Plus, I think if you fell a hundred feet, you'd have more to worry about than some snakes," Leo pointed out. "Broken limbs, crushed skull, that sort of thing."

"Ha-ha."

The guide didn't laugh at that part, either. They'd gone over the rules for this adventure many times; the company prided themselves on their safety record.

"Impossible," the man said, looking offended.

"I know, we wouldn't do it if we didn't think it was safe. It's just, she had a snake encounter at the hotel the other day," Leo explained.

"Oh, then all is well!" he exclaimed. "It is like lightning. You've been struck once, you never will be again."

"Huh." She wasn't buying it.

"He's right, you know. What are the odds?" Leo prodded.

Probably not as good as getting engaged to the tabloid-proclaimed sexiest man alive, yet she'd managed to do that, if only for a very unusual reason.

"Come on, are you really going to let a phobia about something that probably won't happen stop you from doing something you really want to do?" Leo asked.

When he put it like that, it did seem crazy.

"I'll go first if you want, clearing the way."

"My hero."

A grin lifted a corner of his mouth and one of those sweetly sexy dimples appeared. Leaning closer, so the guide wouldn't overhear, he whispered in her ear, "The faster we get back down to earth, the sooner we'll be back at the hotel with those pretty new scarves you bought at the bazaar."

Her heart sped up. The bus had made a couple of stops during the trip here, including one at an open-air market. She'd found a stall selling long, beautiful silk scarves and had bought a few of them, knowing when Leo's brow shot up that he knew why.

"All right, all right. I guess I'll do it."

"Are you sure?" Leo asked, searching her face carefully, all kidding aside. "If you really don't want to, I'll understand."

She gazed at the canopy—all that green—at the zip line extending as far as she could see toward that waterfall, which sounded absolutely beautiful, and nodded. "I'm not going to let a phobia deprive me of something I've wanted to do for a long time."

"Good girl."

Pressing a quick kiss on her mouth, he stepped to the edge of the platform. Within a moment, he was gone, flying like a bird, whooping as he went, his laughter floating back to her on the air.

"Ready *señorita?*" the guide asked.

"Ready as I'll ever be."

She stepped to the edge, took a deep breath and did what she'd been doing ever since she met Leo Santori.

She leaped feetfirst into adventure.

LATE IN THE DAY, after their jungle excursion—which Madison had loved in spite of herself—they boarded the tour bus for the trip back up to their resort. The bus was crowded with other tourists. They'd met some very nice people from various parts of the world. Now, though, after a day with them, she really just wanted some alone time with Leo.

She kept thinking about that beautiful waterfall, and how much she would have liked it if they'd had it all to themselves. Making love in the water, she had recently discovered thanks to her private pool, was one of her favorite things. She could only imagine how it would have felt to stand beneath those cascading sheets of cool liquid and lose herself in his strong arms.

She suspected every other couple there had had the same thought. Unfortunately, nobody'd had the nerve to say, "Hey, how about we take turns, you guys go explore the jungle and give us a half hour." It wasn't like college when they would know by the sock hanging on the doorknob that it wasn't safe to come back yet.

Tucked together on the bus, she and Leo kept their voices low, not talking a lot to the people around them, who were well on their way to being drunk. It was a long drive and the rum punch was complimentary. There was also a guy playing a guitar up front, tourists shouting out windows and being a little stupid. But here in the back, cocooned as they were in their own private little nook, she was able to forget any of them were even there.

"That was pretty spectacular today, wasn't it?" Leo said.

"Definitely."

"Glad you went for it?"

"I am. Thank you for doing it first and scaring the wits out of all the snakes so they got out of the way before I arrived."

"Just call me Saint Patrick."

She sipped her drink, which was heavy on the rum and light on everything else. Half of one was knocking her on her butt, and she couldn't imagine how the people closer to the front, who'd downed three or four, were feeling.

Or, actually, considering they'd had to pull over once for some guy to get sick, maybe she could.

"So, tell me about these Santori men raised by Santori women."

"Huh?"

"You said something about it the other day. About how men in your family learn to treat women right."

"Well, they do," he said with a shrug. "I've told you there aren't many breakups in the family."

"Except for Great-Uncle Rocco and Great-Aunt Gertrude," she said with a laugh, "who got tired of waiting for each other to die."

"Actually, their names are Vinnie and Sarah. But like I said, they're the exception, not the rule. My parents have been married thirty-five years, my dad's brothers even longer. Uncle Anthony and Aunt Rosa just celebrated their fiftieth. All six of their kids, who are happily married, celebrated by giving them a trip to the old country."

"Old country?"

"Italy." The dimple flashed. "I'm Italian, if you didn't notice."

She giggled. Big, brawny, dark-haired, dark-eyed, sexy as hell. Oh, yeah, she'd noticed.

"Are they all Italian? I mean, the wives and everyone?" she asked, hoping he wasn't hearing a question that was dancing around in her brain. That question being—*is one-eighth Italian, by virtue of having maybe an Italian great-grandparent somewhere in the family tree, good enough to get the welcome mat put out by the family?*

She wasn't exactly hinting that they might end up married, but she also wouldn't mind if this vacation fling turned into something more when they got back stateside. She was pretty much homeless right now, and not tied down anyplace, who was to say she couldn't check out the Windy City and decide to stay?

"Definitely not," he said. "Tony's and Nick's wives are—they're also sisters. But most of my other cousins didn't go looking for 'traditional' wives."

She thought, *Good.*

She said, "Interesting."

Although he'd mentioned it, they hadn't talked a lot about his broken engagement. He didn't seem to be dwelling on it, that was for sure, and she hoped it wasn't a sensitive subject. She wanted to know more.

"What did they think of the *former*-future Mrs. Leo Santori?"

It took him a second to process the question and figure out what she was asking. Once he had, he grinned. "My brothers hated her."

"That's not a good sign."

"I know, right? Rafe, my older brother…"

"Army Ranger?"

"Right. He only met her once and told me that she reminded him of a crocodile—big, bright teeth, always ready to bite."

She chuckled.

"And Mike…"

"Cop?"

"Right. He said anybody who took six years to get through college for a degree in decorating was an idiot."

She had to agree with that one.

"So what on earth were you doing with her?"

"I don't know, to be honest." Sounding sheepish, he admitted, "This'll seem stupid, but the truth is, I think she just kind of decided she wanted to get married, I was the one she was dating, and I didn't have much say in the matter."

"Oh, poor wittle you."

"Not saying I was blameless, believe me, I wasn't. I floated into it, having seen all my cousins getting married and pushing out the babies. My mother kept hinting that it was my responsibility to get married first since Rafe was in the military."

Oy. Old fashioned, indeed.

"Looking back, her cheating on me—and me finding out—was the best thing that could have happened. Otherwise, I have no doubt I'd be breaking the Santori family record by being the only one of my generation to get a divorce."

That made sense. Heaven knew, Madison had done her fair share of drifting into things because she had nothing better to do at the time. Look at her engagement to Tommy! Sure, she'd been helping her sister, and helping her friend. But hadn't one small part of her decided to do it because she was bored with her life, unhappy with her job, wanting a change?

"On the plus side, I think my near miss has cooled my mom's jets for a while. She's not going to be pushing any of us anytime soon. Right after the breakup, she called my brother Mike and said, 'Michelangelo, you bring home a girl who spends more money a month on makeup than on food and I'll smack you in the head.'"

Laughing, she said, "Your brother's name is really Michelangelo?"

He shrugged. "Yep."

"And Rafe?"

"Raphael," he admitted.

"Leo…short for Leonardo?"

"Uh-huh." He sighed heavily. "You can say it."

Bursting into laughter, she said, "Your parents named you after Teenage Mutant Ninja Turtles?"

"That's certainly what all my friends thought, growing up."

"They must also have thought you had the coolest parents in the world."

"Well, with that, and my uncle Anthony's famous pizzeria, I didn't lack for friends."

His self-deprecation was cute. The fact that he was a hell of a guy, nice, smart and funny, didn't seem to enter into the equation.

"Truth is, my grandparents emigrated and were very traditional, and my parents wanted to please them. So they went with really traditional names."

"Would there have been a Donatello?"

He shook his head. "Don't think so, though Donato was on the short list when they named Mike."

She twined her fingers with his. "So, Leonardo, huh? That makes you the lead turtle—smart, always has a plan and fights with two Japanese katana swords… cool!"

Lifting a brow in surprise, he said, "You do know your turtles."

"What can I say?" She wagged her brows up and down. "I was into dangerous males from a very young age."

"But not reptiles."

She thrust her bottom lip out. "Turtles aren't reptiles...are they?"

"Amphibians, I think."

"Whew!"

"For what it's worth, I bet those dangerous males were into you, too." His brown eyes gleamed with approval as he stared at her, and she saw his lids drop a little. She had no doubt he was thinking wicked, sultry things, and she wished this bus would hurry the hell up.

He lifted her hand and brought it to his mouth, brushing his lips across her knuckles. His tongue flicked out to taste her—just a tiny flash of moisture—and she quivered in her seat.

"Did I mention that Leonardo was always my favorite?"

He squeezed her hand once more as he lowered it. "Glad to know it. I'd hate to have to katana my brothers' asses if you decided you preferred a hotheaded fighter type like Rafe or a wise guy like Mike."

"Not a chance."

She preferred him. Just him. Over any other man she had ever known.

"We'll be there soon," he said, reading her mind.

As if realizing they both needed to focus on anything other than the cloud of sexual awareness building between them, he went back to what he'd been saying. "So, was your sister a Turtles fan, too? I thought girls preferred Powerpuff Girls."

She laughed out loud. "That's so funny, I was just thinking about those characters!"

"I suppose only people our age would have any idea what we were talking about."

"Nickelodeon generation."

"Exactly. Are there any other ways in which you and Candace were different?"

"She was always very sweet."

A slow, sexy smile. "You're sweet."

He didn't say it, but she knew that somewhere in his mind, he'd reworded that sentence and added the word *taste*.

"I meant well behaved. She was the good girl."

"Making you the bad one?"

"Let's just say I was the one who found all the squeaky floorboards in our house and knew how to avoid them when sneaking out. And was almost always the one who instigated a twin-swap whenever there was a test I wanted to get out of that I knew Candace could do better on."

"Lucky!" he said. "I look a lot like my brothers, but not close enough that either of them could ever bail my ass out when it came time for the next English exam."

Before she could reply, they noticed the bus was stopping. Madison glanced out the window, surprised to see they were still on the road. A long line of cars and trucks were lined up ahead of them.

"What's going on, man? What's the holdup?" one of the passengers asked.

One of the tour company reps, who'd been checking his phone for information, replied, "Angelina and Brad are in town at a charity event! Miles of traffic."

She assumed he meant Jolie and Pitt. Funny how superstars needed no last name, even when in a different country.

"So, you want to stop by and say hi to Brad and Angie?" Leo asked. "You run in their circles, right?"

She snickered. "Not exactly." She'd spied the couple from a distance once at a premiere Tommy had taken her to, but hadn't gotten anywhere close to them.

"But you will be someday."

"You don't know that," she said, wishing the whole topic of Hollywood hadn't come up. That brought back issues she'd been trying very hard to run from this week.

"You never have told me what your screenplay's about," he said. He leaned against the window of the bus in their double seat, turning slightly to face her. His hair was windblown, his face tanned and flushed, his eyes sparkling after their exciting day.

"You don't really want to hear about that," she said.

"Yeah, I really do."

Well, she might not want to discuss why she'd fled Hollywood, but she did like talking about her work. She was proud of her project, protective of every word she'd written, and found herself wanting to share some of that with him. "It's a dark thriller about sexual obsession and murder."

His eyes popped.

"Sorry you asked?"

"Uh, no." He grinned broadly. "As long as you're not here doing research on the murder part of the story."

"No. Just the sex part. Thanks, by the way. I'll be sure you get an acknowledgment in the credits."

"My mom'll be so proud."

"Oh, I'm sure all your friends will line up to see it."

"What will my title be? Maybe gripper. Or best boy." His dimple appeared as he loaded the movie tech terms with innuendo. "I've always wondered what that person did on a movie set."

"It's key grip, not gripper, and *you* don't grip, you caress."

His voice low, he said, "And? What else do *I* do?"

She dropped hers too. "You stroke."

"And?"

"And squeeze."

"And?"

"And pound, and thrust, and kiss, and lick, and hold and…"

He lifted his rum punch to his mouth and took a sip. "I shouldn't have started that."

"No, you probably shouldn't have."

He dropped an arm across her shoulders, tugging her closer so she rested against him. Gently squeezing her, he said, "We haven't talked about this, but…"

"Yes?"

"Well, to be honest, I don't know how I'm going to leave here without you on Monday."

Hearing a note in his voice that said he wasn't finished—and that he might have been thinking about something they could do to remedy the this-was-a-vacation-fling-and-we'll-never-see-each-other-again thing, she said, "I know." Then, thinking a little more, she blinked. "Wait, Monday? You mean, tomorrow?" The idea horrified her.

He appeared puzzled. "No, I mean Monday...four days from now. Today's Thursday."

"No, it's not."

"Uh, yeah, babe, it is."

Not totally believing it, she grabbed the backpack in which she'd carried her wallet and some other stuff from her purse. She found the small calendar that went with her checkbook and looked at it, counting back the days since she'd left California.

He was right. It was Thursday. Good lord, she'd been traveling so much in recent weeks—from L.A. to Napa to Florida to Central America—that she'd totally lost track of not only where she was, but *when* she was. How bizarre!

"See?"

She nodded slowly. "That's so weird, I completely messed up the days. I have no idea why I was so sure today was Sunday."

Of course, it could have been more than the travel and the jet-lag. There'd also been the matter of the stress, the tears, the long, sleepless nights, the races with the paparazzi. All of which had been the driving forces in her life until she'd come here and met *him*.

So yeah, it must have been all those confusing things that had led to the screwup in her internal clock.

But something was niggling at the back of her mind. Some small detail or memory that told her there was more to it. She just couldn't grab the thought, and it was irritating her. She swiped a hand through her hair, loosening the ponytail that had begun to give her a bit of a headache, and tried to focus, but nothing came to mind.

"So, now that you know what day it is, can you tell me how long you're staying?"

"I guess until Monday also. I booked for a week."

Or, well, Tommy's travel agent had booked her for a week. She thought.

It was late in the evening, which meant they had only three more full days. That didn't sound like very much time at all.

Part of her wanted to ask him if he could stay a little longer—if they gave up one of their rooms, perhaps they could put it toward extending their stay.

Another part wanted him to make the suggestion.

You can't hide here forever. You've got to go home and straighten your life out before you can take this thing much further.

"You're sure?" he asked her. "You might want to double-check your reservation."

He was teasing, but only just. And she realized he was right. "I know. At least, I *think* it was a week. This trip was planned on the fly and I've been pretty out of it, obviously."

"Remind me to never let you be in charge of the scheduling calendar."

Scheduling calendar.

That thought whizzed by again. Suddenly, she wrestled it into coherence and when it formed in her brain, she gasped.

"What?"

She didn't answer, bending over to grab her backpack again, worry overwhelming her. *No, you couldn't have been that stupid, right?*

"Madison, what is it?"

She kept digging, looking for a small, hard plastic case. Casting quick glances up at him, hating to admit what was going through her mind, she said, "I had a thought about why I might have had my days mixed up. If I'm right, the bus is going to have to pull over for *me* to throw up this time because I feel just sick about it!"

His worried expression told her he was concerned only for her, not for himself, not for any repercussions. He didn't get what she was worried about.

Hell. If her suspicions were correct, there could definitely be some repercussions for them both.

"What can I do?"

"Pray."

He gaped, obviously seeing how frightened she really was.

Finally, she found the object she'd been looking for and pulled it out of her backpack.

Her birth control pills.

"Are those…"

"Yeah."

She gulped, flipped the lid with her thumb and studied the dial of pills. She was very careful, every month, to set the starting day correctly, because she'd had problems with the pill in the beginning. And there had been that one pregnancy scare in her high school years that she had never wanted to repeat.

According to this package, those pills, and the little days of the week imprinted above them, tomorrow she should be taking Monday's pill. That was why she'd thought today was Sunday.

Only, today was Thursday.

For a second, she prayed she'd taken them ahead of time, too many instead of too few. Crazy hopes blossomed within her and she sought frantically for an explanation. *You took extra protection for all the extra sex, right?*

But she knew she hadn't done that, not consciously, anyway.

Leo had obviously been studying the case, too. His brow was furrowed, his expression serious. "What's the verdict? Are there too few or too many?" he asked, jumping to the same conclusion.

She thought about it. Last week she'd been in Florida, the week before in Napa. She'd started this package of pills while she was still in L.A.

The days rolled out in her mind, and by the time she'd finished calculating them, she realized she was in trouble.

"There are too many pills left," she whispered. "Three more should be missing. So I have apparently missed three doses at some point over the past few weeks."

He was silent. She was silent.

Dropping the plastic case into her backpack, she

threw herself back in the seat and closed her eyes, her mind swimming with confusion.

Three pills. Three little pills. That couldn't be a catastrophe, could it? She'd been on the pill for ten years. After all that faithful service, surely one minor mistake like this wouldn't result in…couldn't mean she was…

"So you could be pregnant."

He'd put it right out there, voicing the words she'd been unable to even think. She flinched, slowly lowering her glass of rum punch and putting it into the drink holder in her armrest. She told herself it was instinct—that she felt queasy. But she couldn't deny that something, some tiny spark of oh-my-God-what-if-it's-true, had thought *this isn't good for the baby.*

"No. Of course not," she insisted. "It's crazy."

He wasn't in a panic and he wasn't angry. Not happy, certainly, but not reacting the way she'd expect most twentysomething single men to react to the news that they might have knocked up a woman they'd met a few days ago.

"It's possible, though."

She gulped and slowly nodded. "I'm so sorry, Leo. It's been… I'm *never* so careless. I've just had an awful few weeks, my mind's been spinning. I screwed up. I totally screwed up."

She finally worked up the nerve to open her eyes again, knowing there were tears in them. Blinking rapidly to hold them back, she looked at him, dreading his reaction. Maybe his was a calm before the storm.

But oh, that warmth, that understanding in his expression. If she'd been standing, she would have lost her legs and fallen to the ground, so overwhelmed was she by the tenderness in his handsome face.

"Shh, it's okay," he insisted. "Stop beating yourself up about it. I'm sure it won't happen. The odds are crazy."

"Right."

"Worse odds than encountering two snakes in Costa Rica."

She forced a chuckle that came out a little like a sob. "Yeah. Of course they are."

He lifted her across the seat onto his lap, wrapping his arms around her and pulling her head onto his shoulder. His hand gently stroking her hair, he said, "It's okay, Madison. It'll be fine."

"I can't believe you're not freaking out."

"Over a mistake that anybody could make that *might* lead to a bigger problem? Why would I freak out over that?"

Amazing. She didn't know any other guy who wouldn't have already started losing it, or stated his stance on abortion, or accused her of dumping pills into the toilet to trap him, or at least calling her careless.

This man was unique and so wonderful. Aside from that, he also calmed her, steadied her. She'd always been told she was too volatile, that she had a temper, that she could be thoughtless at times.

Leo was everything she wasn't. He was like a port in a storm, soothing and so damned strong. She wondered if there was any crisis he couldn't weather, and acknowledged that, God forbid this slipup of hers resulted in pregnancy, she couldn't imagine anyone better to go through it with.

"If there's something to worry about, let's deal with it when it happens," he said, brushing a kiss across her temple. "In the meantime, let's just make sure we stop in my room when we get back to the hotel so I can grab some condoms."

She tried for a real smile. "That's a deal." She promptly ruined that with a big, sad-sounding sniffle.

"And maybe a blue necktie. I can tie holes in it and tie it around my face, and maybe get some fake katanas and *really* be your hero."

The smile was a little more genuine this time. "You already are."

They were silent for another moment.

Finally, he said, "It's really okay. It'll be fine, Madison. Let's not worry about it until next month."

Next month. They hadn't even exchanged phone numbers, yet Leo was assuming they would still be… something. She really believed he thought they were going to have some kind of future after this Monday.

Oh, she hoped so. She most certainly hoped so. Because, no matter what day of the week it was, or how many weeks it had been, she was falling for Leo Santori. Falling head over heels, out-of-her-mind, crazy-in-love with him.

She might have come here to escape and to hide.

Now, she suspected she'd been found…and didn't want to be lost ever again.

10

THEIR THREE DAYS left together flew by way too fast for Leo's liking.

Once Madison had stopped beating herself up about what might happen due to her mix-up with her pills, she'd let him coax her back into a good mood. He'd done it with lots of laughter, long walks on the beach, midnight swims in their private pool, surfing lessons, a wind-sailing expedition, dancing at the club of a big touristy resort nearby. And lots and lots of sex.

Damn, he didn't think he would ever have another week like this in his entire life. And he knew he'd never had one before.

They didn't talk about the birth control pill issue, instead using condoms as a matter of course. He wasn't thrilled about it—having been inside her warm, wet body, skin to skin, he really disliked there being any kind of barrier between them. But there was no sense in taking risks.

Although, to be honest, part of him wasn't sure he minded so much.

Yeah, it was crazy to be thinking about having a kid with a woman he'd met a week ago.

But yeah, he was thinking about it.

Whatever he'd thought about his life, his future, his relationships or his prospects before coming here to Costa Rica didn't matter a damn. Because, since he'd met her—since he'd begun to fall in love with her—he was seeing whole new worlds of possibility. Worlds that included him and Madison, committed, together, bringing more little Santoris into the world. No, he wouldn't have chosen to do it so soon, but he wasn't going to deny that, if it happened, he wouldn't be absolutely devastated.

He just wanted to make sure that Madison wanted him as much as he wanted her…and that, whatever happened between them, *didn't* happen only because of a possible pregnancy. That was why he hadn't pushed her for any confirmations on where things would go after they both left this wonderful place. But now it was Sunday night. And in the morning, they were both going to leave this wonderful place.

It was their last night in paradise, but rather than going out somewhere, they'd decided to have a room service dinner. The hotel might be small, but the chef was outstanding, and, once again, they were served an amazing meal.

They shared it outside on her patio at a small table draped with a snowy-white cloth and lit by a few tapered candles. Again, the staff had gone overboard. He had no doubt word had spread that his bed wasn't being slept in—while hers usually looked like a troupe of monkeys had been doing acrobatics on it all night long.

"What are you thinking about?" she asked.

"Monkeys."

She tilted her head, visibly curious, but he only laughed.

"What about you? What are you thinking about?"

"I'm thinking I want one more naked swim in that pool."

He shifted in his seat.

"And wondering how long we'll have to wait until room service comes to take all this stuff away."

He dropped his napkin onto his plate, reached for his water and finished it, as well. Although they had never even discussed it, neither of them admitting any reason for it, he'd noticed that neither he nor Madison had been drinking any alcohol during the past couple of days. It was as if she were already protective of the life that might be growing inside her. And he… Well, he wasn't sure whether it was solidarity or a desire not to jinx anything, but he was laying off, too.

"There's a Do Not Disturb sign on the door. The waiter offered to put it there and said we can just call when we want them to come back," he said with a suggestive wink.

"Do we need to wait a half an hour after eating before we can swim?" she asked.

"I don't think so, considering the water's not even over our heads."

"Perfect," she said, already rising to her feet and pushing at the straps of her sundress. They fell, revealing those soft shoulders, and then the whole dress dropped with a whoosh.

She hadn't been wearing anything underneath.

He swallowed hard, staring at her, awed, as always, by that perfect body, so curvy and feminine. She was lightly tanned all over, no lines to mark the infrequent presence of her skimpy bathing suits.

"Come and get me wet," she said, throwing him a sassy look.

He played along. "The pool's not too cold this time?"

"Not talking about the pool," she promised.

"Good."

He pushed back from the table and stripped off his clothes, grabbing a condom from his pocket before letting his shorts hit the patio. Madison watched him, her eyes zoning in on all the places on his body that she seemed to like a lot.

He was already as hard as a rock.

"Okay, never mind, I don't think I need your help. I'm already there," she exclaimed with a visible quiver of excitement. She clenched her thighs tight, as if to catch the moisture building between them, and his mouth went wet with hunger.

"I think I should check and make sure."

He walked to her, dropping the condom on the pavement right beside the pool, knowing there would be a lot to do before he would want to put it on. He slid his hands around her waist, stroking her hips, pulling her to him. She tilted her face up and their mouths met in a warm, lazy kiss. Their tongues twisted and mated, each stroke languorous and hungry, each breath shared, their heartbeats falling into the same rhythm.

When they finally broke apart, she whispered, "Thought you were going to check it out."

He nodded. Hiding a grin of mischief, he wrapped his arms more tightly around her and jumped into the pool, bringing her with him.

She came up sputtering, splashing his face with water and swimming away. "That was a dirty trick."

"What? Now I'm positive you're nice and wet."

"Maybe not everywhere."

"Everywhere," he said, totally confident.

"Wouldn't you like to know."

He stepped toward her, enjoying the coolness of the water against his naked skin. "Yeah. I would like to know."

She stopped moving away, her teasing words dying on her lips, as if she knew, as he did, that their time together was too short to delay. They wanted—needed—each other, tonight more than ever, and all the playfulness evaporated. There was just intense heat, and, he suspected, a hint of desperation. They both knew they had to leave in mere hours.

Madison watched Leo approach, and saw the same note of, not sadness, but maybe wistfulness on his face that she sensed was on hers. Saying goodbye to this man would be next to impossible, and frankly, she didn't want to think about it. Not when she still had him for a little while longer.

They came together, their bodies meeting beneath the surface. She loved this sensation, had loved it from the first time they'd swum naked together. Water caressed her, cooled her, even as his slick skin warmed and aroused her. There was no weight, no gravity to combat, and they could float and thrust and twist and love to their hearts' content, wrapped in their own wet world.

"I'm going to miss this," she admitted.

"Me, too."

"Not many opportunities for skinny-dipping in Chicago?"

He didn't smile. "Nobody I'd want to do it with if there were."

Madison sighed a little, loving that admission.

"This has been the best week of my life, Leo," she said, reaching up and wrapping her arms around his neck.

He encircled her waist and held her tightly against him. Bending to kiss her, he replied, "Mine, too."

The kiss was sweeter, soft and tender, and in it Madison read a lot of emotions neither of them had expressed. Although she wanted to express them now, to let him know she longed for so much more than this, she knew she couldn't. There was too much to deal with, too much to fix in her life, before she asked him to be a more permanent part of it.

Not that she was about to let him go completely. God, no. She just wanted to be able to come to him with a clean slate. She longed to admit to him exactly what she'd been running from and why. Until that time, telling him she cared about him—hell, that she *loved* him—seemed unfair.

After the kiss, he said, "Are you cold?"

"No."

He lifted her higher as he dropped lower in the water so he was eye level with her breasts. "You look cold."

She laughed softly. "*So* not cold."

"Maybe I should warm you up, just in case."

"You do that."

He did, lapping up some of the water off the curve of one breast, kissing his way toward its tip. He breathed a stream of warm air over the puckered nipple, and then covered it with his mouth and suckled her.

She threw her head back, groaning with pleasure. Lifting her legs, she wrapped them around him and floated there, rubbing herself against his heat, indulging in all the sensations battering her body. His mouth on her breast, his hand on her hip, another twined in her hair, his big, thick cock between her legs, brushing against her core.

There was nothing better than this on earth. Nothing.

He moved to her other breast, pleasuring her just as thoroughly, and then began to draw her back toward the steps at the end of the pool. She saw the condom lying on the pool deck where he'd dropped it but wasn't ready to lose all that hot male skin just yet.

When they got to the steps and he reached for the packet, she said, "Wait."

He eyed her quizzically.

Giving him her sultriest look and licking her lips, she said, "Sit on the top step."

One brow rose. He did as she asked.

Kneeling below him, most of her body still in the

water, she kissed her way up his powerful leg. The wiry black hairs teased her lips as she nibbled and tasted her way ever higher.

He dropped a hand onto her shoulder and tangled the other in her wet hair, obviously knowing where she was headed. When her cheek brushed the side of his erection, he jerked a little. And when she ran the tip of her tongue all the way from its base to its tip, he groaned out loud.

"Madison…"

"I love how you taste," she admitted, licking the moisture that seeped from the tip of his cock.

"Jesus," he groaned.

He liked it, she knew that much. She'd loved doing this to him at various times this week, but they'd never done it in the pool. And the position was so easy and so perfect, the steps lining up exactly the way she needed them to be.

Opening her mouth as wide as she could, she sucked the thick head of his cock.

His guttural groan told her he liked what she was doing, as did the gentle squeeze of his hand on her shoulder. She slid her mouth down, taking more of him, filling her mouth with him, licking the salt and the chlorine and the *male* right off him.

When she could go no farther, she began to pull away, sliding up, knowing her pace was both a torment and a delight. Another flick of her tongue as she lapped up more of his body's delicious juices, and she went down again. Up and down, slow, then faster, soft, then harder, until her jaw hurt and Leo was thrusting a little with every stroke.

"Enough," he said with a gasp. "Get up here."

She wanted to finish, wanted to swallow him down, but she was also dying to have him inside her. So with one last powerful suck, she released him and kissed her way up his stomach, tracing his abs, licking his nipples, biting his neck.

"You definitely should hold the world record for *that*," he said before sinking both hands in her hair and dragging her mouth to his.

He kissed her deeply, thanking her with every thrust of his tongue, releasing her only so he could grab the condom. Tearing it open, he sheathed himself and then pulled her onto his lap. She straddled him, her knees beside his hips on the step.

Another kiss, deep and hungry, but also incredibly tender, and he began to ease his way into her. She took him, every inch of him, every breath of him, every ounce of him, grabbing and holding and loving and savoring. Wanting all of him. Wanting this memory to imprint itself on her very soul so she would always be able to return to it and relive such glory.

When they were fully joined, as close as they could be, she looked into his eyes—those beautiful brown eyes—and said all the things she couldn't yet say aloud.

She'd swear he said them back.

REALITY RETURNED WITH a vengeance the next morning. As if to punctuate the regret both of them were feeling, Leo awoke to the sound of rain. It was the first time they'd seen anything but a blue sky, and the weather suited his mood.

They were both ass-dragging, having stayed up way too late last night indulging in a long, lethargic lovefest that had left him weak but utterly satisfied. Because of that, they'd overslept a little.

Not wanting to suffer the long drive all the way back to the airport in San José, Madison had been able to get a ticket on a puddle jumper that would take her from Liberia, the same airport from which he was flying, to the capital. That meant they had a little more time together. During that time, he intended to ask her when they were going to see each other again.

He'd prefer tonight in Chicago. But it seemed pushy to ask. So he would have to settle for the weekend.

She'd admitted she wasn't working on anything right now except her screenplay, and he knew she was between permanent homes, though he'd never found out exactly why. She'd said she was heading back to her parents' place in Florida while she regrouped.

Chicago was a very good place for regrouping, if he did say so himself. Plus, flights between there and Florida were pretty cheap. Hell, if she couldn't come to him, he'd go to her.

When they reached the airport and checked in, they hesitated before going through security. Their gates were far apart and they had some time before their flights would start boarding, though his was earlier than hers.

Sitting together in a bar in the main terminal, each of them drinking a Virgin Mary, he said, "So. Madison."

A tiny smile tugged at the corners of her mouth. "So. Leo."

Their eyes met. He knew she knew what he was about to say.

"Facebook?" she asked.

He barked a laugh. "I'm not on it."

"You're joking!"

"Sorry, I prefer regular media to the social kind. I like actually knowing people I call friends."

She nodded in commiseration. "I guess I understand that. And I was just kidding since I don't have a profile anymore, either."

"Really?"

"I got rid of it once I started getting too much attention."

"Because of your screenplay?"

She nibbled her bottom lip and hesitated, staring at him searchingly. It looked as if she wanted to say more, and he wondered if she was finally going to reveal just what she was running from.

The fact that she was running, and that she'd gotten rid of her Facebook profile because of too much attention, suddenly made a sharp fear stab into him. *Had she been stalked? Was she on the run from an abusive ex?*

His hands fisted on the table, but he covered by reaching for his drink.

"Something like that," she finally whispered.

He knew it wasn't the whole story. But he also knew she wasn't ready to tell him the whole story.

"Just tell me one thing. Are you in any kind of danger?"

Her jaw fell open. "Oh, God, no, of course not."

"Okay then."

"It's…it's complicated," she admitted.

"I hear ya. It's all right. I can wait, though not forever."

"You won't have to, I promise."

Good. Her secret would give them plenty to talk about when they saw each other back home. Tonight or next weekend or next month. Hopefully no longer than that.

"So I guess we'll have to do this the old-fashioned way," he said, trying to lighten the mood. "You're hot. Can I have your phone number?"

Her green eyes twinkled and she replied, "Well, I don't usually give my number out to strange guys…"

"Hey, I'm not strange. Just Italian."

A broad smile. Thank God. "Okay, I *guess* it's okay if you call me." She reached into her carry-on and pulled out her cell phone. "Tell me yours so I can punch them into my address book."

He rattled off his numbers—home, cell and the station, and threw in his uncle's restaurant just to be on the safe side. She was laughing and complaining about sore fingers by the time she'd finished entering. After she was done, she raised an inquiring brow.

"I hate to admit it, but we're gonna have to do this the *really* old-fashioned way. I didn't get an international SIM card, and knew my phone wouldn't work here so I never even took it out of my suitcase."

"Which you already checked."

"Right."

"I'll text them to you."

"No way. I don't trust technology when it comes to something this important. Write them down."

"Okay, but I don't want to hear any excuses about you losing my number," she said. "Remember, I have yours and I can stalk you and be all vengeful if you give me the brush-off."

He reached across the table and took her hand. "Not gonna happen, Madison Reid. That is *never* gonna happen."

Their gazes met and held and he knew that, once again, they were saying a *lot* more things that didn't really need to be verbalized. In utter silence, they were thanking each other for the amazing week they'd shared, and promising each other it would be continued. They were admitting there were feelings and promising they would be explored. All without a word being spoken. Just like when they'd made love in the pool the night before.

Without ever even opening his mouth, he'd told her he loved her. He even suspected she'd heard it. And that she felt the same way.

Someday soon they'd say it out loud.

"Here you go," she said, pushing a small sheet of paper across to him. It contained a number marked "cell," and another marked "parents in Florida."

He carefully folded the paper and tucked it into his wallet, right next to his license and certification cards. No way would he lose it. Hell, he'd probably be digging it out to call her within an hour of landing at O'Hare.

They finished their drinks, not saying much, both

stealing glances at the clock. Until, finally, knowing he couldn't delay any longer, Leo got up and held out a hand to her. She rose, too, sliding up against his body. He felt her, even though an inch of air separated them, vibrating with life and passion. He felt her magnetism even when they weren't touching.

"Soon," he demanded, a wave of want washing over him, the way it always did when she was near.

She nodded. "Soon."

Before he could say more, they were startled by raised voices. A large crowd of people had gathered at this end of the terminal. They stood right outside the bar, which was open-air, separated from the main section of the airport by only a half wall. That might explain why it was so damned loud.

He hadn't been paying attention, but now all those people—most carrying cameras—came to life and began shouting questions and snapping pictures. "What the hell?"

"Angelina and Brad are flying out this morning!" someone at the next table whispered, peering around and out into the main terminal.

He rolled his eyes, not interested in the celebrity stuff and only hoping the rolling out of the red carpet didn't delay his flight.

Hell, what was he thinking? This could go ahead and delay it indefinitely, as long as Madison's was delayed, too. Of course, with their luck, they'd each be on their respective planes when the delay happened.

"Think they're following us?" he asked her, laughter on his lips.

It died when he saw her expression. Her eyes were wide and glassy, her mouth rounded in shock. She was staring at the crowd gathering a couple of yards away and he could actually hear her harsh exhalations as she struggled for breath.

"Mad, what is it? What's wrong?"

"Oh, my God," she whispered. She spun around, burying her face in his neck, hugging him tightly and mumbling, "We should go."

"You going to walk backward?" he asked, placing a gentle hand on the small of her back.

She looked up at him and now he didn't just see shock, he saw something that resembled panic. "I mean, you should go. They'll be boarding your flight any minute," she said, suddenly jerking away from him and giving him a push. "I have a little more time."

He couldn't understand her sudden change in mood, but she was right. They would be calling for his flight soon and he still had to get through security.

"If I didn't know any better, I'd say you were trying to get rid of me."

"I shouldn't have come here with you," she said, casting quick glances over her shoulder. "I should have taken a cab to the other airport." She looked at him, her eyes wide and wet. "I never dreamed they'd find… Oh, Leo, please forgive me. I was being selfish, I just wasn't ready to say goodbye. Now I've exposed you to…"

"Madison, whatever it is, it's okay," he told her. Dropping his hands to her hips, he pulled her close, so their bodies touched from thigh to chest, and dropped his mouth onto hers. He kissed her deeply but gently, saying goodbye and reminding her of all the things they'd be missing until they saw each other again.

He usually didn't make out in public, but kissing Madison always made him a little crazy. He deepened things, liking how she clung to him, kissing him back, wildly, hungrily.

They didn't break apart until they heard someone calling her name.

"Madison!"

Then another voice.

"Over here, Miss Reid!"

And another.

"Is he the guy, Madison? Is this where you've been all this time?"

"Any chance you and Shane will reconcile?"

"What's going to happen to the house you two were sharing in California?"

Looking down at her and seeing the utter misery in her face as she grabbed a sun hat and glasses and pulled them on, he could only stare.

"What's your name, buddy? Where are you from?"

"Are you the one she cheated with?"

"Come on, Madison, lay another kiss on him! The world wants to know who you prefer to Tommy Shane!"

Tommy Shane? The movie star?

His heart stopped and his stomach flipped. The room suddenly seemed to spin and it had nothing to do with the heat. He found it hard to think, hard to see, hard to process much of anything except those voices and those snapping cameras.

And the guilt on her face.

"Madison...?"

"I'm sorry. I'm so sorry you got dragged into this, Leo," she whispered, tears falling from her eyes. "I didn't want this to happen to you, I'd never wish it on my own worst enemy, much less..."

Those awful, intrusive voices continued, digging into his brain like sharp, spiky instruments. "Madison, how did you two meet? When did the affair start? How'd Tommy find out?"

Affair. Tommy.

God.

The pieces started to come together in his mind. Tommy Shane—everyone on the planet knew his name. And while he didn't pay attention to Hollywood gossip or junk like that, he now remembered having heard something about a breakup. He'd been visiting his cousin Lottie. She'd just had her second child and he'd glanced through some gossip rags someone else had brought her to look at while nursing.

She'd gone on an indignant rant about poor sweet sexy Tommy Shane, wondering how any woman could cheat on him. A woman who'd been *engaged* to him.

This woman. The woman he suddenly wasn't even sure he knew.

She'd been engaged to one of the most famous men in America. *She cheated.* She'd been hounded by paparazzi. *She cheated.* She'd fled to Costa Rica. *She cheated.* And put another notch on her bedpost?

She cheated.

Every instinct he had rebelled against the idea, but he could think of no other explanation. She wasn't screaming at these people that they were liars. She looked utterly ashamed. Guilty as sin.

His sweet and sexy Madison had betrayed the man she'd promised to marry and had used Leo to lick her wounds while the scandal died down. It was the only thing that made sense.

What he couldn't figure out, though, was what had happened to her lover. Considering she'd lost Shane over the man, he had to be pretty damned important. Which made Leo wonder what the hell she'd been doing slumming around with *him* for the past seven days. She'd cheated on a man who women threw themselves in front of.

So why had she just spent a week here with him, a regular guy?

"Leo, please, let me explain," she insisted, raising her voice to be heard over the paparazzi.

"How about starting with the basics. Were you engaged to Tommy Shane, the movie star?"

She nodded slowly.

He thought he'd been prepared for the answer, but considering he thought he was going to puke, he guessed he hadn't been.

"You lived with him. That's why you're between addresses now."

"Yes."

It got better and better.

"And you came here to get away from all the bad publicity you were getting because of your breakup."

"Yes, but you don't understand," she said.

His whole body rigid, he stepped away from her.

"Speak up, I'm sure everyone would love to hear the story."

She closed her eyes, shaking her head in sorrow and regret.

He wanted to shake her, wanted to yell at her for lying to him.

Only she hadn't, not really, except by omission. She'd never said anything about a broken engagement or an affair. She'd kept her secrets well. He'd just been stupid enough not to see the truth.

Again.

Christ, what was it with him picking women who couldn't be faithful? Was it some character flaw he had?

Part of him screamed at the very idea of putting Madison in the same category as his ex. But in the end, they weren't much different, were they? In fact, Madison's affair had been a whole lot more public.

"I've gotta go," he said, trying to be heard as the photographers and reporters who'd struck out getting the good stuff on Brad and Angelina pressed inside the bar and swarmed them like flies on meat.

"Yes, you should, get out of here before this gets worse."

"It can get worse?"

"You have no idea," she said, her tone bleak.

He was angry. Furious, in fact. He wanted to walk out and leave her here to deal with her own mess.

But he just couldn't do it. He couldn't walk away and leave her in the middle of this feeding frenzy to be chewed up by these animals, even if a part of him thought she probably deserved it.

"Come on," he ordered, grabbing both their carry-ons. He dropped a possessive arm over her shoulders and pulled her along with him, elbowing people out of the way with every step.

The barrage continued.

"Just tell us your name!"

"Do you have anything you want to say to Tommy? Do you feel bad about stealing his woman?"

"Are you two living together somewhere?"

He ignored them. So did she. Together, fighting for every step, they pushed through the crowd. Leo threw a few elbows at those who wouldn't move voluntarily. Finally, they reached the security area, through which nobody without a boarding pass could come. He waved theirs and jerked a thumb toward their pursuers. "I don't think they're passengers, and they're harassing us."

The guards immediately stepped in, ushering them into a secured line, leaving the crowd behind. Still the shouts continued, and Leo could practically feel the cameras taking pictures of the back of his head.

That finally struck him. It wasn't just the shock and betrayal of her not being who he thought she'd been. He'd now been dragged into this. His picture was going to be plastered on their tabloids, his name, his home, his job, his family…everything was going to be thrown out there for public consumption if they found out who he was.

Fuck.

"Thank you," she said as they finally turned a corner and got out of sight of the crowd.

He immediately dropped his arm and stepped away from her.

"If you can, please keep my name out of it, would you?" he bit out from a granite-hard jaw. "I don't imagine it would go over very well with my lieutenant or with my family."

"I'm so sorry," she whispered, watching him, tears falling freely down her face. "I never imagined that would happen, not in my worst nightmares."

He'd heard enough. He just couldn't listen to any more. So when they reached the end of the first line and he saw that there were several checkpoints, each with its own separate queue, he watched her go into the closest one…and headed for one as far away from hers as he could get.

He told himself it was because it was shorter and his flight would board soon.

He knew the truth, though. He needed to think and to breathe. Needed to absorb everything that had happened in the past ten minutes and figure out what it meant and what he was going to do about it.

He needed to get away from her.

"Leo," she said as he turned his back and began to walk away.

He didn't turn around, not trusting himself to look at her face. Instead, he called, "I can't, Madison. Not now. I just can't."

And he didn't. He didn't look back. He didn't wait for her. He didn't try to find her at her gate.

He simply got on his plane and went home.

11

MADISON MADE THE trip home like a zombie, barely cognizant of her surroundings. She'd been able to focus only on the look on Leo's face when he realized he'd been thrown into the deep end of the ocean by a woman he'd thought he could trust.

Her father picked her up at the airport in Florida. As soon as he saw her by the baggage claim, he pulled her into his arms, hugging her tightly. "I'm so sorry, baby girl. So sorry, honey."

She clung to him, feeling tears well up further.

"It didn't help, huh?"

Had her trip helped? Well, the majority of her week hadn't just helped, it had been downright magical. But the ending had been like something out of her worst nightmare.

"I'm okay, just tired," she said, knowing he would see right through it. Her emotions were spinning wildly, and if anybody would recognize that, it was her wise, attentive father.

"Listen, why don't I get your bag? You duck behind

the escalators, I'll grab the suitcase and go get the car.
Once I've pulled up to the front, you can dash right out."

Distressed that he had to go to these lengths, especially considering his recent heart attack, she said, "I
shouldn't have come here. I should have just gone back
to California."

"Forgedaboutit," he said. "Come on now, get on over
there. I've always wanted to play James Bond."

"Did you bring weapons?" she asked, heavy on the
sarcasm.

"No, but I brought a new secret-agent-mobile that
none of those cockroaches will recognize."

She gaped. "You got a new car?"

"I wanted to be less noticeable when you came back.
Traded in the old jalopy." His smile said that hadn't
been a hardship.

"You got the SUV you've been bugging Mom about."

"Yup." He hugged her again. "Thanks for the crisis, honey."

Knowing he was trying to cheer her up, she forced
a laugh.

"Oh, and if it's okay with you, we're going to head
over to the condo instead of the house."

Her parents lived inland, but had bought a place on
the beach as an investment years ago. She supposed
it was possible they'd planned a beach trip, but she
doubted it.

"The reporters drove you out of your house?"

"Are you kidding? You know your mother. She's
gotta have those ocean breezes. Can't keep her away."

Probably an exaggeration, but she didn't call him on

it. Her parents were doing what parents did, taking care of their kid in her moment of need. Even if the kid had screwed up royally by getting in a situation she hadn't been prepared for and making a decision she'd pay for until the end of her days.

She wasn't just the woman who would go down in infamy as the cheater who'd broken Tommy Shane's heart. She'd also lost the one man who'd ever made her feel as though she was capable of loving someone with every fiber in her being.

"I'm glad you're here," her dad said. "You can pay me back for the ride by making me one of your chocolate cakes…your mother tries to sneak zucchini and wheat germ into hers."

"Ick," she said with a soft laugh, then murmured, "Thanks, Dad."

Their plan worked. He picked her up outside and she didn't hear anyone demanding answers that were nobody's business. They arrived at the condo, which was gated, making it difficult for them to be harassed if anyone tracked her down.

Nobody did. And for the next several days, Madison began to heal.

There was never a sign of a photographer, and while she saw the photos of herself and Leo on the cover of a tabloid at the grocery store, she didn't see his name. She prayed they hadn't discovered who he was, and so far it appeared their luck was holding.

She couldn't imagine how he was explaining it to his colleagues, or anyone in his family, but hoped they were trustworthy enough not to sell him out to the *Tattler*.

Her mother had seen the pictures, too. They'd been standing in line at Publix, and her mother's gasp had cued her in. But being just as supportive and protective as Madison's dad, she didn't say a word. She instead reached up and *accidentally* spilled her cup of iced coffee on the cover of the tabloid.

She hadn't even asked Madison to explain who it was she'd been kissing in Costa Rica, as if realizing the hurt she was feeling might have more to do with that than with what had happened out in L.A. Not for the first time, Madison acknowledged she had the best parents in the world.

She was loved. She knew that. She'd never doubted it. And out of the spotlight, at the small beach town, she began to find peace, to think about her future and figure out what to do.

Calling Leo had been on her mind a lot. A whole lot.

She couldn't begin to count the number of times she had picked up her phone, looked at his numbers in the address book and thought about dialing.

Would he answer? Would he listen? Would he hang up on her?

Did it matter?

Because, even if he would listen, how could she explain? She couldn't tell him the truth without revealing the nature of her engagement to Tommy. Couldn't drag Tommy out of the closet to someone he didn't know when he'd tried so hard to stay in there for the rest of the world. She had seen her sister go through the exact same dilemma when Candace had fallen in love. She'd just never thought it would happen to her, too. Who could ever have imagined a Leo coming into her life?

Besides, he obviously didn't want to talk to her. She kept her phone nearby but he never called. She checked for messages even though it didn't ring. But nothing. He hadn't tried to reach her.

She didn't blame him. He was too decent a guy to be dragged into her garbage. She should never have let herself forget that.

Sitting on the balcony of the condo, watching the waves churn one evening after she and her parents had shared dinner, she began to drift off to sleep, lulled by the ocean and the call of the seabirds. In that lazy place between asleep and awake, she replayed all the lovely moments the two of them had shared.

Their first meeting. The room mix-up. The lovemaking on the beach. The stupid snake in the pool. The zip-lining tour. The long bus ride back when they'd talked about a lot of nothing.

A lot of...*nothing.*

Her eyes flew open. "Oh, my God," she muttered.

"What, honey?" asked her mother, who'd been sitting nearby doing a Sudoku puzzle.

"What's today?" she snapped.

"Thursday, why?"

Thursday. Of course it would be Thursday. Wasn't it always freaking Thursday? "Do you know the date?"

Her mother told her, and Madison started calculating.

She'd been in Florida for seventeen days. She could hardly believe it. Apparently, she'd been so numb, she hadn't noticed the passage of time. Each lazy day had rolled into the next, none bringing a solution to her problems or offering a glimpse of happiness with the man she missed so terribly.

Seventeen days.

That day on the bus with Leo, she had figured out when she'd started her last pack of pills. The date was emblazoned in her mind and it wasn't hard to count backward to see just how long it had been: six weeks ago.

She was late. Two weeks late.

Calm down. It might not be that. Could be stress, anything.

But Madison was never late—she hadn't been in years. Besides, something deep inside her already knew the truth.

She was pregnant.

Pregnant by a man who obviously never wanted to see or hear from her again for the rest of his life.

"What's the matter, Madison?" her mom repeated.

She couldn't tell her folks—not because they were old-fashioned or wouldn't be supportive, but because she just couldn't drag them into even more of her drama. None of this was their fault; how could she add to the worry that was already making her mother so sad? Put more stress on her father's recovering heart?

"Sorry, Mom, I just remembered some stuff I need to take care of." The next words left her lips without her giving them much thought. "In California."

Her mother didn't look surprised, as if she had already come to that conclusion herself and had just been waiting for Madison to figure it out. "All right, honey."

Yes, it was time to go back to California and deal with this once and for all. With a baby to consider—and she truly believed there was one—she could no longer be the story-of-the-week for the cheap news mags. She would be in no position to run around evading the paparazzi.

Besides, she was a fighter, not a quitter. She was good-and-damned tired of having her life ruled by strangers dying to find out sordid details that were not their concern.

She had to see Tommy—and Candace, who she needed now so much her heart ached—and figure out what to do. It was time to reclaim her life. Maybe by doing so, she could go to Leo and tell him the truth.

She hoped he would not only listen…but that he could deal with the fact that he was going to be a father.

"HEY, BRO, HOW'S it going?"

Leo heard his brother Mike's voice, but didn't slide out from under his truck. He continued with his oil change, wishing his brother would go away but knowing he wouldn't.

"You gonna come out or are you hiding?"

"Bite me," he muttered.

"I did when we were four and six. You gave me a fat lip."

"And mom spanked me," Leo said, smiling reluctantly.

"So are you coming out?"

"If you're here to pump me for information, forget about it. I don't want to discuss it."

"Can't a guy just stop by on his lunch hour to say hello to his brother?" Mike squatted down beside the truck, peering at him. "Seriously, I'm not here to bust your balls. I was in the neighborhood and just wanted to see how you're doing."

He sighed heavily. "Give me a minute." At least Mike hadn't come over here to rag on him about the pictures in the tabloids like the guys at the station did.

It had been a crazy couple of weeks.

He'd been *in a mood,* as his mother would describe it, since the minute he'd left Madison at that airport in Costa Rica. The flight stateside had been miserable. He'd vacillated between anger, regret and humiliation the entire way.

Things hadn't improved much once he got home. His family and friends had noticed, but he hadn't told them anything. He was still too raw, too unsure what to believe, to talk about it.

Once the heat of anger had died down and he'd really begun to think, he'd realized there was no way he knew the whole story. First, he didn't think anybody was a good enough actress to pretend the happiness Madison had seemed to feel when they were together. She hadn't behaved at all like a woman pining for another man— her ex-fiancé *or* her mystery lover.

Second, everything inside him rebelled at the idea that she was the type who would cheat. She didn't come across as anything less than an honest person. The moment he'd met Ashley, he'd seen that tiny hint of selfishness that had made it less of a surprise that she couldn't be faithful. He'd never seen that in Madison. Never.

Besides those factors, he also couldn't stop thinking about one of their first conversations, the one when she'd said she hadn't had sex in six months. That hadn't felt like a lie. Besides, why would she make it up? There would be no need for her to invent a detail like that.

But if it were true…what did *that* mean?

That she was innocent and hadn't cheated?

That she hadn't slept with her fiancé—the sexiest man alive, per magazines—since long before they'd broken up?

Confusion didn't begin to describe the state he'd been in. Finally, knowing he had to get the answers or go crazy, he'd pulled out the slip of paper with her phone numbers on it. It had been late, and he'd been leaving the station after a long twenty-four-hour shift. But he hadn't wanted to wait until morning, knowing that in the light of day, when he was less fatigued, he might rethink the decision.

No answer. He hadn't left a message, instead deciding to try the other number for her parents' house in Florida.

It had been disconnected.

Well, if she really had gone back to their home after the nightmare in Costa Rica, he could understand why the phone was no longer connected. Hell, if the paparazzi figured out who he was and where he lived, he'd not only want to change his address and phone number, he'd want to change his damn face!

The very next day, when he'd been about to try to call her again, the story had broken. Those leeches had published the pictures from the airport. He was officially being called "the unidentified man who stole Tommy Shane's fiancée."

And his life totally went to hell. Everybody saw it, everybody commented on it. He was able to laugh off what he called a "resemblance" to people he didn't know. Those he did know, who were aware he had, indeed, gone to Costa Rica, weren't buying it.

"You need a hand?" Mike asked.

"No, I'm done," he said as he finished tightening the filter. Double-checking the seal, he slid out from under the truck and sat up. "Bring any beer?" he asked his brother.

"I'm working."

"I'm not," he said, enjoying the first morning of his long, three-day stretch off. Rising to his feet and wiping his hands with a rag, he added, "Come on in."

Before they turned to walk through the garage into Leo's small house, Mike dropped a hand on his shoulder. "You holding up?"

"I've been better."

Mike followed him inside, and Leo went to the fridge to grab himself a beer and his brother a bottle of water. Going into the living room, they sat down and eyed each other in silence for a minute.

"So, heard from Rafe lately?" he asked, wondering how their older brother was doing. An Army Ranger stationed in Afghanistan, their other sibling didn't communicate much. The whole family was anxious for him to finish up his tour of duty and get the hell out of there.

"No, not a word. Mom's hoping he'll make it home for Christmas."

"Think that'll happen?"

"I doubt it."

They fell silent again, and Leo knew his brother had something else on his mind. This wasn't just a stop-by-to-say-hey visit.

Finally, Mike spoke. "Have you heard from her?"

Leo merely stared, surprised by the question. It was the first time anybody had asked him that. Most of his friends just ragged on him, trying to get information out of him, asking what it had been like to bang a movie star's ex. His family pretended it hadn't happened, changing the subject, not wanting any details.

Nobody had even asked how they'd met, what they'd done, or how he felt about her. *Really* felt.

"No."

"Have you tried calling?"

"I did before the pictures hit the press."

"And she hasn't called you?"

"I didn't leave a message. The last time we spoke at the airport, I made it pretty clear I didn't want to talk."

"Harsh, dude."

His jaw stiff, he admitted, "It wasn't my finest moment."

"I guess you had provocation."

Maybe. Or maybe he'd just been a jerk, acting like the injured party when he really didn't know what was going on. He should have at least given her the chance to say something—anything. He'd been on autopilot, in shock, operating on instinct and emotion. And he regretted it.

"Was it pretty serious?"

He nodded slowly. "I thought so." Swallowing, he admitted, "To be honest, Mike, I was picturing marriage and babies and all that crap, right up until the minute the press showed up."

His brother leaned forward in his seat, dropping his clenched hands between his splayed legs and hunching over.

"What is it?"

"There's something you should know."

His heart skipped a beat. "About Madison?"

Mike nodded. "And maybe about you." He reached into the pocket of his jacket and pulled out a folded piece of newsprint. "Mom saw this article this morning and asked me to come talk to you. She wanted you to hear it from one of us."

Leo reached for the paper, unsure why his mouth had gone so dry and his heart was beating so fast. Unfolding the square, seeing it was a torn-out page of a tabloid, he felt a little sick, but forced himself to look at the "news" article anyway.

At first, the words didn't make sense. As they began to sink in, though, the world seemed to stop spinning, then to suddenly lurch wildly. He spun with it, unable to do anything but stare at the words on the page.

Who's the Daddy, Madison?

He scanned the article, crumpled the paper in his hand, looked up at his brother and said, "Get me to the airport."

"ARE YOU OKAY?"

Madison awakened from a light nap as her sister

stuck her head into the bedroom, offering her a gentle smile. Candace had flown down the day before yesterday, a few days after Madison had returned to California. They were both staying with Tommy in Laguna Beach.

"I guess," Madison mumbled. "I'm just tired all the time now."

"I suppose that's to be expected," her twin said, entering the room and sitting down on the corner of the bed. Although Candace was concerned, there was also a gleam of excitement in her eyes. Ever since she'd found out that Madison was pregnant, she'd been torn between being upset for her and being utterly thrilled that she would be an aunt in about eight months.

That was now official. The three pregnancy tests she'd taken since she'd arrived in California confirmed it.

She was pregnant with Leo Santori's baby.

"You aren't feeling nauseated or anything, are you?"

She sat up, leaning back against the pillows. "No, not really. A tiny bit queasy in the evenings, but mostly I'm just tired." She rubbed at her eyes and asked, "Where's Tommy?"

"He and Simon are downstairs making dinner."

"Are the shades drawn?" she asked, sounding bitter.

They really didn't need to worry too much about that behind the gates of this secluded mansion. Tommy had bought it for privacy, after all. The front lawn was large and gated, the house set well back from the road. The backyard comprised a steep, rocky hillside that led down to the beach and nobody but a goat could climb it. So, yeah, her comment had just been sarcastic. The paparazzi might be cruising the street in front of the house, but they weren't snapping embarrassing pictures, the way they had when she'd first arrived at Tommy's place a week ago and run the gauntlet to get to the gate.

She hadn't had the stomach to read any of the articles or watch the Hollywood "news" shows since her return. She knew full well everybody was speculating that Tommy, being the great guy he was, had taken back his cheating ex-fiancée.

"I need to talk to you. It's about the press."

"Screw them all," Madison muttered, unable to help it.

Candace reached out and took her hand, which Madison had noticed was actually a bit pale, despite her tan. She suspected she'd lost a little weight and knew she wasn't getting enough exercise. She'd been practically hibernating, consoling herself in the company of her sister and her best friend as they all brainstormed on how best to deal with this.

Tommy had offered to marry her. Same old knight in shining armor. Simon, his partner, hadn't seemed too thrilled about it, but hadn't objected. He knew full well how Madison's life had been shredded because of all of this.

Madison had of course declined. It wasn't the 1950s—she didn't need a father's name on the birth certificate. If there was a name to put on there, she wanted it to be the real one. She only hoped that by the time she'd gotten things straightened out here, Leo would listen to her when she showed up in Chicago to break the news.

This wasn't the kind of thing she could say on the phone, so she'd already bought her ticket. She was leaving in two days. Tommy had told her to tell Leo anything she had to in order to make him understand the truth of the situation. He'd offered to go with her. Hell, he'd offered to hold a press conference to stage a big coming-out party.

All she'd really needed was that permission to share his secret. She didn't want him throwing himself on his sword for nothing. Her real hope was that by staying here with him for a few days, maybe the press and the public would see she and Tommy were still friends. Maybe they'd begin to believe she hadn't broken his heart, that their engagement had just been a mistake.

Maybe they'd let her get her life back.

Get Leo back.

"Mad, something's happened. Mom called this afternoon."

Hearing the note of anxiety in her sister's voice, she gripped her hand tighter. "Is Dad all right? His heart…"

"He's fine. It's just… I don't know how to tell you this."

So it had something to do with *her.* "Just say it."

Candace swallowed. "The *Tattler* has a big story about you."

Oh, great. "What else is new?"

"*This* is new. It seems somebody—probably one of their slimy reporters—dug through Tommy's trash the day after you arrived."

Slimy indeed. She hoped he'd gotten a handful of fish guts.

"Mad, he found the test kits." Candace's hand tightened. "Your pregnancy's all over the tabloids."

She froze, unable to process it, hoping her sister was joking. But Candace was dead serious—the tears and sympathy in her eyes proved it.

"You mean they printed…"

"Yeah. Big headline, nasty article, lots of speculation over who the father is." Candace drew her into her arms and held her tightly, as if fearing Madison was about to break apart.

Funny, though, as the immediate reaction died down, she realized she wasn't devastated, wasn't furious. Mostly, she was just terrified. *What if Leo saw it?*

"I've got to go!" She launched out of the bed. "I have to change my flight to Chicago."

Candace nodded. "I'll call while you pack."

But before they could do either, the intercom in the room buzzed on. Tommy loved the stupid thing and played with it all the time. "You awake?"

"I'm busy."

"Mad, you have a visitor."

"No time," she snapped, wondering who on earth would be coming to see her, and, more importantly, why Tommy would let them in.

"He's coming up the driveway right now. Get your ass down here!"

"He who? What are you talking about?" she asked, finally paying attention.

"A gorgeous Italian guy who demanded to be let in,

and then flipped off a dozen photographers in the street as he drove through the gate."

She gasped. *Leo?*

"Do you think it's him?" Candace asked.

She considered, thought about the articles, remembered the conversation they'd had. He would know the baby was his.

"It's him," she whispered, her hand rising to her mouth as she dashed over to the dresser to check her face in the mirror. "Of course, I haven't bathed in two days and I look like a red-eyed raccoon with these bags under my eyes."

Candace leaped to the rescue. She quickly grabbed Madison's makeup bag and touched up the dark circles. There wasn't much she could do about her hair, so she slung it into a ponytail. It took only a minute or two, but even that was too long.

She hurried downstairs, her heart racing, arriving at the bottom of the steps just in time to see Leo Santori throw a punch at her former fiancé. Fortunately, Tommy ducked to the side and evaded the shot.

"Stop, Leo, don't!" she shouted.

He jerked his attention toward her. His dark eyes studied her, his gaze sweeping over her, from messy hair down to bare feet. She saw the tiny furrowing of his brow and knew he didn't like what he saw. She hoped it was because he was worried about her and not because she looked like total shit. Or because he hated her guts.

"This isn't Tommy's fault," she said immediately, trying to diffuse the tension. "And the papers have everything all wrong."

"Are you pregnant?" he snapped, cutting right to the issue at hand.

She nodded slowly.

"Is it mine?"

Another nod.

His bunched shoulders relaxed a little and the dark frown eased. He didn't exactly look overjoyed about the news or ready to pass out cigars, but at least he no longer appeared about to beat the crap out of Tommy.

"So you're not going to deny it, try to claim it's his?" he asked, jerking a thumb toward Tommy.

"Why would I do that?" she asked, genuinely puzzled.

Candace had followed her downstairs, and Simon had come in from the kitchen. He ignored them both.

"I don't know, Madison, I don't have any idea what you might be thinking. But I do know one of those fucking articles is saying lover boy here can't have kids so you went out and had an affair only so you could give him the baby he wants."

Her legs went weak as dismay washed over her. How could people invent such horrible, vicious lies? She lifted a hand to her forehead, suddenly feeling light-headed.

"Mad?" Tommy said.

Leo didn't speak. When he saw that her weakening limbs were about to betray her, he launched himself forward and caught her in his arms. She fell into them gratefully, inhaling his unique scent, feeling the heat of his body and finally allowing herself to believe he was really here.

And then, for the second time in her life, she fainted.

12

LEO DIDN'T KNOW his way around this gaudy California mansion, so when he realized Madison had passed out from shock, weariness or the pregnancy, he simply strode through the nearest doorway, hoping there was a soft surface on which he could place her.

It turned out to be a dining room. The rich wood table was as big as his own kitchen. Jesus, had Madison really been living like this?

"In here," Shane said, gesturing toward another doorway.

Glaring at the man, not wanting his help with anything, Leo nonetheless carried her into the other room. Spying a large plush sofa, he gently lowered her onto it. "Get her some water and a cold cloth."

"Here." Someone thrust a wet facecloth toward him, obviously having gone for it the moment she'd fallen. He glanced up long enough to realize it had been Madison's twin sister, Candace. He nodded his thanks, thinking she might be identical in features, but she certainly didn't make his heart dance around in his chest the way it did when he looked at Madison.

He placed the cloth on Madison's brow, not liking the paleness in her face and the circles under her eyes. She looked like she hadn't slept at all in the weeks since he'd seen her. There were hollows in her cheeks that hadn't been there before, and her hands and arms looked so much smaller and more fragile than he remembered them being.

"Madison, sweetheart, wake up," he whispered.

Her eyelids fluttered. A pause. Then they flew open. "It's really you. You're really here."

"Yeah. Did you think it was a dream?"

She nodded. "It wouldn't be the first time."

So she'd been dreaming about him? Well, that was only fair, wasn't it, considering she'd inhabited his dreams and his fantasies every day since he'd walked away from her at that airport?

"You haven't been taking care of yourself," he scolded.

"You're not looking so great yourself." She lifted a slender hand and brushed her fingers across his lips. "You've lost weight."

"So have you. And you should be gaining it, shouldn't you?"

Her hand immediately dropped to her waist. She again displayed that protective instinct he'd already seen when there was just the possibility of a baby.

How could she be a cheat and a liar? How was something like that even possible?

He no longer believed it was. Which was why he'd

gotten on that plane this morning, right after Mike had shown him the article, and flown out here to get to the truth.

"I was coming to tell you," she said, as if reading his mind. "I have my tickets booked."

"Really?"

"Really," she assured him. "The confirmation is in my purse. I was coming in two days. I never wanted you to find out about the baby like you did."

"Okay," he said, believing, because, as always, he could sense no deceit in the woman.

"I'm so sorry you had to read about it in the damned tabloids. That's so wrong."

"It's all right. They're like piranhas, aren't they?"

"Wish you'd run a few of them over when you flew through the gate," said the world's sexiest man.

Leo stared up at him, his expression hard and unyielding. Although the rest of the world was boo-hooing about poor Tommy Shane and his broken heart, Leo knew—*knew*—there was more to this whole thing. Madison was the one who'd been hurt. She was the one who'd been nearly crushed by the weight of all this, and he believed she deserved it about as much as he believed in the Easter Bunny.

"Ooh, fierce," Tommy said. He held his hands up, palms out, in a conciliatory gesture. "Take a breath, big guy."

"What the hell is going on?" Leo asked, looking away from Tommy and down at the woman trying to sit up on the couch. He put a hand under her arm and helped her. "Explain this to me because I've read all the stories and the gossip and the innuendo, and I don't believe a word of it. So somebody needs to start talking."

Madison glanced first at Tommy, and then at the other man, who was dark haired, well dressed and standing close to the famous actor. Then at her sister. "Would you excuse us, please?"

They all immediately mumbled apologies and scurried out of the room, leaving them alone.

Leo ached to reach out and pull her into his arms, to hold her again, this time while she was conscious. He held back, though. They had to clear the air and he didn't want to make this any harder than it was already going to be.

"I've missed you so much, Leo," she said. "I've thought about you every minute of every day."

He dropped onto a nearby chair, surprised those had been her opening words, though he certainly echoed the sentiment.

"Wow. I hadn't planned to start off like that," she said, swiping a hand over her brow. "I'm not trying to manipulate things, gain your sympathy or anything."

He didn't reply, still savoring that admission, still wondering what was yet to come.

"Tommy Shane and I were engaged, but we were never planning to get married. He's been one of my dearest friends all my life, and that's all we have ever been to each other, and all we ever will be."

About twenty pounds of weight lifted off his shoulders. But a lot more remained.

"So why the engagement?"

She gestured toward the window. "You think they're

ruthless now? Imagine what they'd say if word got out that the hottest action star in the country...is in love with a man."

The lightbulb clicked. The presence of the dark-haired guy made sense.

Leo closed his eyes and dropped his head back onto the chair, letting out a heavy sigh. It was as if somebody had set a domino in motion and all the other pieces began to fall down, one after another, everything sliding into place.

When he thought his voice wouldn't shake, he said, "You were his beard."

"Exactly. It wasn't supposed to last forever. And when he got serious with his partner, we decided the time had come to break up. Only, we needed a reason. A really *good* one."

"Why?"

"Because what woman in her right mind would break up with the sexiest man alive? Unless he did something horrible. Which would really take a chink out of that superhero-of-Hollywood image."

Right. Nice guys didn't cheat. Not when they had relatively new careers *and* a big secret to hide.

"So you pretended you'd had an affair."

She nodded.

"*You* took the fall, carried the burden for weeks while he...while he..."

"While he offered to come out in the open, to throw away his career and his life and his privacy," she said gently. "Tommy's heart is breaking for me. *I'm* the one who won't let him make this more of a spectacle than it is."

Spectacle. Yeah, that pretty much described the life she'd been living lately.

"To be honest, I also didn't want to let those bastards win. Why should they get their way?" She punched the seat cushion. "Why should they be free to hound people to death, prying in their closets, and under their beds and…and in their trash cans!"

He'd read the articles about her pregnancy and knew where that information had come from. How low did somebody have to be to dig stuff out of the garbage? He supposed only someone who wallowed in it for a living.

"I never thought it would be such a big deal…slow news month, I guess."

"It's not news," he snapped. "It's gossip and slander and they're all sick, miserable people with black souls, no lives, and…small penises."

She smiled weakly, nodding in agreement.

"You went to Costa Rica to hide, didn't you?"

"Yes."

"Never planned on meeting anyone, I'll bet."

She peered at him and her voice throbbed with intensity as she replied, "I never expected to meet *you*. Not in Costa Rica. Not anywhere. Not in my whole life."

She was baring herself, laying out her every emotion, exposing herself to more heartache—on top of the mounds of it she'd already been dealing with. All for someone who'd never once told her how he felt about her.

"And I never thought I'd find you, either," he said softly.

Unable to stay away from her any longer, he rose from his chair and sat beside her on the couch. He put his arms around her and gently—oh, so gently—pulled her onto his lap. She wrapped her arms around his neck and tucked her face next to his.

"I missed you, too, Madison."

He couldn't see her smile. But he could feel it.

Maybe they were being cautious, telling the truth, but not telling all of it. What he felt for her was a lot more than absence making the heart grow fonder. He'd missed her, yeah. Because he loved her like crazy.

Unfortunately, they were in someone else's house, with three strangers right outside the door. They hadn't seen each other in weeks. She was exhausted, pregnant, emotionally wrung out.

And she hadn't said she loved him, either.

She does. He knew she did.

But maybe it wasn't quite time to say it yet.

"I'm sorry I didn't come find you sooner."

"And I'm sorry I didn't come tell you the truth sooner. I was going to, I just had to make sure Tommy knew and understood, since it's his secret that's at risk of getting out."

He thought about her friend, considered the life he led. Tommy Shane was an international sensation. He'd risen out of relative obscurity just three or four years ago and had become a superstar. He made millions, lived in a mansion, had women hanging on his every word, turned down movie offers that other actors drooled for…and could never *really* be who he was.

He never would have imagined it, but he truly felt sorry for Shane. It was one hell of a choice to have to make.

"How are we going to get out of this mess, Madison?" he whispered, tenderly kissing her temple. "Because I want it over. I want you in my life and I want our baby."

"I don't know," she admitted. "I honestly don't know."

ALTHOUGH LEO HAD hit it off with Tommy after Madison told him the truth, and also got along great with Candace and Simon, they decided to leave for Chicago that very night. For one thing, he needed to get back to work, having used almost all his vacation time in Costa Rica. And Madison needed to get out of this atmosphere. It was toxic and she knew it was bad for her health, and for the baby's.

More than that, though, she just wanted privacy so she and Leo could spend some time together in the real world. Time to accept all that had happened, to explore the feelings they had for each other and see if they were really as strong as she suspected they were.

They could also use some time to get used to the idea that they were going to have a child together.

They couldn't do that here, certainly. Nor did Leo intend to leave her here, living like a bug under a microscope, while he went home alone.

They'd thought about how to slip away, and it had been Candace who'd come up with an idea—which was why, late in the day, a limousine with blacked-out windows pulled up in front of the house, parking at an angle to help block the view from the road. Each of them wearing a jacket, hat and dark glasses, Madison and Leo said their goodbyes and dashed to the car. The driver let them in, closing the door behind them.

Some of the photographers ran to their cars as if to follow. But before they'd even left the driveway, Candace had come outside, waving enthusiastically at the limo as it departed.

The press stayed. Madison could see the confusion on their faces as they peered at the limo, trying to see who was inside.

Somehow, they'd missed her sister's arrival the other day and had no idea her twin was on the premises. When she'd shown up, they'd probably just assumed it was Madison—that she'd gotten out of the mansion under their noses and was returning.

Whatever the case, the press mistook the sisters for each other again now. Ignoring the mysterious vehicle, they focused instead on the fresh meat standing in the driveway, waving happily, acting as though she didn't have a care in the world.

Madison glanced back, her heart twisting as she saw her brave sister standing there, sticking up for her. Their lives had gone in very different directions, and she doubted they'd ever live in the same state again. But some things never changed—like the instant connection they shared, the way they would drop everything on a dime to be there for each other.

They had each found love with great men. But they would always be twins.

She continued to stare, sending warm, loving thoughts out to her sibling. Suddenly, Tommy walked out of the house. So did Simon. That hadn't been part of the plan. Both of them walked up to Candace, stood on either side of her, and slid an arm around her waist. They laughed together and all three waved, looking like one happy family.

She giggled. "I have no idea what the vultures are going to make of that!"

"Hopefully it'll give them all aneurysms just thinking about it," Leo said, sharing her laughter as he pulled her close on the leather seat, draping an arm across her shoulders.

"I hope my father doesn't have one," she said, shaking her head.

She'd called Florida right before they'd left. Her parents hadn't been thrilled that she'd run away the moment she'd found out she was pregnant. Nor were they happy to have found out about it from friends who read the tabloids. But she'd heard the excitement in their voices and, at the end of the conversation, they'd admitted they were *thrilled* to be having their first grandchild.

"Let me kiss you, woman," he growled. "It's been way too long."

She didn't hesitate. The privacy screen was up. Needing desperately to feel him, touch him and know he was real, she moved over onto his lap, twined her arms around his neck and pulled him close for a long slow kiss. He cupped her face in his hands in the way she so loved—so tender, yet sexy. Sultry but sweet. They kissed and kissed, laughing and whispering between each brush of their mouths.

"I could get used to traveling like this," he said. "Think he'd drive us all the way to Chicago?"

"Sure. We'll send the bill to Tommy."

Chuckling, he kissed her again. "Don't I wish. I do have to go back to work, though."

"Too bad. We could get him to drive us all the way to Florida. My parents are dying to meet you."

"I'm looking forward to meeting them, too," Leo said, sounding sincere.

"They're wonderful. They'll love you." She sighed heavily. "They've known Tommy forever and are in on his secret, so they won't hate you on sight like your folks will me."

She was more than a little terrified about meeting his family, having them think of her as some tramp loathed by the entire world.

"Stop it," he ordered. "They'll love you as much as I do."

She froze. Still, so still. Surprised, happy. Wondering whether he'd meant those words or they were an expression.

Love. He'd said the word *love*. She hadn't misheard it, had she?

As if reading her mind, he lifted her chin so their eyes met.

"I love you, Madison Reid."

Her heart thudded, practically escaping from her chest. That was fine. She didn't own it anymore, anyway. This man did. "You're sure?"

"I've never been more sure of anything."

Slowly nodding, she allowed the truth of it to fill

her up, let it sink in to all those empty places that had been hollowed out by the days and weeks of being without him.

He loved her.

He'd come for her.

He wanted her and he wanted their baby.

She could face anything.

When she was able to speak, she said, "I love you, too, Leo. I am totally and completely yours."

"I know."

She couldn't help poking him in the ribs. "You cocky Italian."

He grinned up at her, that gorgeous dimple appearing, his face glowing with utter happiness. "Come on, what's not to love? I mean, you'll never do better than me, babe. You must've hated life in that huge mansion with the beach and the pool and the art and the movie stars dropping by all the time."

Giggling, she replied, "Oh, definitely. The horrors!"

"I ask ya, what could be better than a little two bedroom house right around the corner from a noisy fire station?"

"Two bedrooms are enough for me."

In fact, it sounded like heaven to her.

She realized they'd both just assumed she would live with him. This didn't feel like a vacation. It was crazy. She'd left most of her things behind in California or in Florida, but it felt like she was on her way home. At last.

As long as she had a computer on which to write and a phone with which to make and receive calls, she could continue pursuing her screenwriting career. If that didn't pan out, well, there was always the *Chicago Tribune,* or another big city paper. Most of them would probably be chomping at the bit to scoop up a journalist with a masters from Columbia.

"Southern California? Who needs it?" Leo asked as they cruised up the coast. "Limos and Porsches and beaches? Screw that. Nothing beats the Windy City. Lake-effect snow, crime, cold that cuts right through your bones."

"Can't wait," she said with a laugh. "I'll be able to take you up on that pizza challenge."

"You'll love my cousin Tony's food. In fact, you'll love the whole family. And they *will* love you. I swear it."

"You really think so?"

"I know so."

"Even if this whole nightmare doesn't die down? We can't just tell everyone the whole story, you know. I'm sorry, that has to be Tommy's decision."

"I understand. But I'm telling you, sweetheart, there's only one thing my mom'll need to hear—that she's going to be a grandmother."

Remembering her own mother's reaction, she believed that one.

"As for the rest, we tell them it's a bunch of sensationalistic lies. That you and Tommy were childhood friends who decided you just worked better as friends, and the tabloids made a bunch of nonsense out of it. Who doesn't know that, anyway? I mean, really, how many martian spacemen have you seen flinging a Frisbee in Central Park?"

Laughing out loud as she pictured some of the more outrageous tabloid headlines she'd seen, she nodded helplessly. "Okay."

Their laughter faded. Growing serious, as if knowing she needed the reassurance, he said, "They're good judges of character, Madison."

"If they're anything like you, I know I'll love them all." She nibbled her lip. "But Leo, sooner or later, the press is going to figure out who you are. Somebody will out us and the maniacs will descend on us, no matter where we are."

He smirked. "Oh, honey, there's no place in Chicago that the Santoris can't block the press in and stop them from getting anywhere near us."

"There are that many of you?"

"I've got more relatives than a new lottery winner— cops, bodyguards, lawyers, construction workers, business owners, strippers, politicians…"

"Strippers?" she said, gawking.

"My cousin's wife. You'll love her. She also bakes— oh, *madone,* you haven't lived until you've tried her cannoli."

"I'll add it to my list."

"The point is, there's a Santori on every corner, and every one of them will serve as a barricade to anybody who tries to mess with one of their own."

Swallowing, she asked, "And I'll be one of their own?"

He brushed his fingers against her cheek, reached for her left hand and laced their fingers together. He lifted it to his mouth, placing a tender kiss on her ring finger.

She knew what he meant. Knew exactly what he meant.

"You already are, Madison. You're mine."

"Forever?"

"Forever. Rings, vows, whatever you want." He bent to brush his lips across hers, sealing the promise with a gentle kiss. "I'm never letting you get away again."

Epilogue

LEO WAS AS GOOD as his word. The family loved her. And she loved them.

Going from a small family with one sibling and only a few other relations into a clan like the Santoris was a bit of a culture shock. Madison was thrown into a whirlwind of aunts, uncles, cousins and in-laws.

It was crazy. It was wonderful. And Leo was by her side through every bit of it.

Although none of them ever made her feel at all unwelcome, or questioned the story she and Leo had told them, she had to admit she felt a lot better after Tommy's press conference.

The one where he'd shocked Hollywood.

No, he hadn't spilled everything, but he'd come pretty damned close. Telling the world that it was wrong for *anyone* to have to feign an engagement with one of his oldest friends, and then see that friend ripped to shreds in public over it, he asked the media to take a good, hard look at themselves.

Of course, the tabloids wouldn't…they thrived on

gossip. But there had been plenty of supposedly "legiti-mate" news outlets that had ripped them apart, too. So maybe his words would do a little good there.

Lots of people speculated that their fake engage-ment, and his demand for privacy, for the right to live the way he wanted to, meant he was gay. But so what? More fans stepped out in support of him than criticized, and a lot of other celebrities had backed him up with similar comments.

His last film had opened at number one and stayed there for weeks. His career was thriving. He was happy—if discreet—with Simon.

And she and Leo were, blessedly, being left in peace.

"How are you feeling?" Leo asked, coming up be-hind her as she typed the last few words of her screen-play. She'd been doing revisions for a studio that had optioned it, wanting to get all the work behind her be-fore their upcoming trip to California.

"I'm fine," she insisted, hearing the worried tone in his voice. He wouldn't stop worrying until their daugh-ter was safely in their arms and Madison had fully re-covered from childbirth.

If there had ever been a more overprotective father-to-be, she had yet to meet him. Absolutely the only time she could persuade him she wasn't about to break, and was perfectly healthy, was when she seduced him into some seriously naughty sex. Seriously. Naughty.

Yum.

It turned out that being pregnant pumped up her li-bido to astronomical levels. She found herself ripping Leo's clothes off every chance she got.

He didn't seem to mind.

"You're sure you're going to be okay to fly? I'm sure Candace would understand…"

"I'm six months pregnant, not on my deathbed," she said, rolling her eyes as they went over this again.

"Six months. Our lucky number, remember?" he said with a suggestive wag of his eyebrows.

"I can't wait to see what happens six months from now next October." Then she got back to the subject at hand. "But as for now, I am *not* missing my sister's wedding. We're going to Napa. End of discussion."

"Bossy chick."

"Hey, what can I say?" She adopted a fake accent and made a hand gesture she'd seen her new father-in-law make many times. "I'm Italian, ya know?"

He broke up over her awful imitation. "Brilliant," he said.

"Hey, I learned from the best. I guess that's why your bossiness has rubbed off on me."

"Baby, you were trying to run the show from the day we met."

Oh, that wonderful day they'd met. How she loved to think about it, and most of the days that had followed, right up to and including their own special, intimate wedding ceremony here in Chicago a few weeks ago.

Well, it had been private, but it certainly hadn't been small. Her family had come, of course, along with Tommy.

And then there had been the Santoris. All the Santoris.

They'd filled the church without inviting a single out-

side guest. A few *un*invited ones had tried to sneak in—
they followed Tommy everywhere he went and were
still looking for dish about Madison. But one of Leo's
cousins, Nick, was a former bouncer and ran a popular club. He'd *bounced* one photographer out on his ass
and the others had scurried for cover.

"So, you're really feeling all right?"

"Indeed I am."

"Then finish that sentence and come to bed."

She glanced out the window at the bright blue sky
and raised a brow. She was only teasing him, of course.
She and Leo had never felt the need to restrict themselves to the dark of night. Their baby had probably
been conceived in broad daylight in a swimming pool
for heaven's sake.

"What's that look?" he asked as he took her hand
and helped her out of her chair.

"Thinking of our last vacation."

He closed his eyes, obviously picturing it, too.
"Guess we won't be able do that again until the kid's
twenty."

Hmm. Maybe not.

They should certainly be able to afford it, anyway.
Her screenplay had not only made a splash, it had made
a tidal wave. Once Tommy had held his press conference, and she'd been the object of sympathy worldwide, the studios had swooped in and fought like dogs
over her work.

She supposed she could have felt a little offended,
could have thought about it as a pity bidding war.

But screw that. She cashed the check.

"Maybe we can take her with us and go when she's three or four," she said. "I think she should learn how to swim naked."

He nodded, liking the idea. "As long as she's potty trained."

"Good point."

They were laughing together as he bent down to pick her up. He often did that, sweeping her into their bedroom. She thought she might cry on the day she became too heavy for it and told him so.

"Never gonna happen."

"I'll be big as a house in three months."

"I'll eat my Wheaties." He pressed a kiss on her cheek, on her nose, then a long, lazy one on her lips. "Because I learned a long time ago…when I'm holding you in my arms, I can do absolutely anything."

* * * * *

Want more Santoris? Watch for
A SOLDIER'S CHRISTMAS,
coming in December, from Harlequin Blaze.
Rafe Santori is going to make it home to Chicago
no matter what…he just isn't prepared to run
into a woman from his past who makes the trip
a whole lot more exciting.
And watch for Mike's story next year!

No Desire Denied

"In one of my books, this would be a plot point. The characters would have to make a decision. Either they find out and deal with the consequences or they keep thinking about it. I would assume that in your job, it pays to know exactly what you're up against. Right?"

"Close enough."

But *he* wasn't nearly close enough. The heat of his breath burned her lips, but she had to have more. And talking wasn't going to get it for her. If she wanted to seduce Reid, *she* had to make the move.

Finally her arms were around him, her mouth parted beneath his. And she had her answers.

His mouth wasn't soft at all, but open and urgent. His taste was as dark and dangerous as the man. That much she'd guessed. But there was none of the control that he always seemed to coat himself with. None of the reserve. There was only heat and luxurious demand. She was sinking fast to a place where there was nothing but Reid and the glorious sensations only he could give her. She wanted to lose herself in them. Her heart had never raced this fast. Her body had never pulsed so desperately. Even in her wildest fantasies, she'd never conceived of feeling this way. And it still wasn't enough. She needed more. Everything. Him. Digging her fingers into his shoulders, she pulled him closer.

Big mistake.

In some far corner of Reid's mind, the words blinked like a huge neon sign. They'd started sending their message the instant he'd told her they would settle what was happening between them now. He'd gotten out of the car to gain some distance, some perspective. Some resolve. But the brief respite had only seemed to increase the seductive pull Nell had on him.

He'd been a goner the moment he'd stuffed himself back into the front seat.

Long before that.

Oh, her argument had been flawless. Knowing exactly what you were up against was key in his job. Reid heartily wished it was her logic that had made his hands streak into her hair and not the feelings that she'd been arousing in him all day.

For seven years.

The hunger she'd triggered while she'd been talking so logically felt as if it had been buried inside him forever. Then once her lips pressed against his, he forgot everything except that he was finally kissing her. Finally touching her hair. He hadn't imagined how silky the texture would be. One hand remained there, trapped, while the other roamed freely, moving down and over her, memorizing the curves and angles in one possessive stroke.

Pick up NO DESIRE DENIED by Cara Summers, available October 22, 2013, wherever you buy Harlequin® Blaze® books.